DAVID NETH

HEAT

DUST STORM

Book 2

DN Publishing

Dust Storm
Heat, Book 2
Copyright © 2019 by David Neth
Batavia, NY

www.DavidNethBooks.com

ISBN: 978-1-945336-66-9
First edition

Subscribe to the author's newsletter for updates and exclusive content:
DavidNethBooks.com/Newsletter

Follow the author at:
www.facebook.com/DavidNethBooks
www.instagram.com/dneth13

Prologue

The basement of the Ellsworth Institute of Technology is quiet. Nearly empty of all people. The only sound is the one lone custodial worker sweeping up a mess in room B120. Mitchel Derrick Mantel.

That's good.

A second person slowly makes his way down the staircase, careful not to make any loud noises to alert Mitch. That wouldn't be good. However, from what he's noticed from other times they've had encounters, Mitch likely has headphones in, completely oblivious to what surrounds him.

The newcomer isn't like that. He's been planning this move for almost a week now. Finally, without all the hubbub of freshmen orientation, student move-ins, and the first week of classes, things have just begun to settle into a familiar routine around campus. It's the perfect time.

But the plan isn't ideal. It'll work, but it's a line he didn't think he'd have to cross. He never thought he'd end someone's life. It's the only way, though. Especially after he'd developed these unusual powers.

They're extraordinary.

They make *him* extraordinary.

They make him powerful.

He isn't really a religious man, but it's hard to ignore the fact that these powers—that came right when he needed a solution the most—is a sign from God. Suddenly, it's as if the path in front of him is lit, pulling him in this direction.

But this plan doesn't come without flaws. He could be spotted. He could fail to kill Mitch. He could leave some sort of trace that he was the one who ended this man's life.

Still, it's a risk he needs to take. Mitch took what's most important to him and for that, he needs to go away.

Turning from the final step on the staircase, his foot bangs the side of the metal railing, sending echoes across the empty basement.

Dammit.

Rushing to hide behind a wall, he manages to duck out of sight before he can be spotted.

"H-Hello?" Mitch's voice calls out.

He waits quietly, anxiously, for Mitch to give up and go back to work. The plan can still be executed.

"Hello?" Mitch calls again.

Silence.

"Is someone there?" the worker calls again.

More silence.

Chancing a look down the hall, he sees that Mitch has finally returned to B120 and he breathes a sigh of relief. But the hard part isn't over.

Closing his eyes, he enacts his power. The next moment, he no longer occupies a complete physical form. Instead, he's several physical forms, working in unison, hovering above the ground.

PROLOGUE

Rounding the corner, he moves to the door of B120 and hovers just outside, watching as Mitch maneuvers the mop around chair legs and under desks. White cords hang out of each of his ears, confirming that he's listening to music.

He hovers just inside the hallway and waits. He wants to see the terror on Mitch's face. See the realization come over him that his life is going to end. It's the justification he deserves for Mitch ruining his life.

Mitch turns and works his way up the walkway on the other side of the room, behind a large island counter in the middle with electrical cords hanging from the ceiling. He glances up once, then twice, seeing what's waiting for him in the hallway.

He strikes, rising up into a growing cyclone that fills the room and sends papers and other loose articles flying from the desks.

Mitch steps back and watches wide-eyed as the cyclone grows, multiplying until it consumes the room.

The look alone gives him satisfaction, but it isn't enough. Mitch is still breathing and he can't have that.

Mitch needs to die.

Eyeing up the distance to the door, Mitch races toward it, tripping over his mop bucket on the way. Just as his hand grasps the doorknob, though, the cyclone envelopes him.

Reluctantly, Mitch breathes in the sand—it *lunges* at him—and he collapses on the ground in a coughing fit. The attacker doesn't relent, forcing the particles he's become down Mitch's throat until his meager attempts to breathe subside and the room is quiet once again.

Chapter One

With a coffee in each hand, I make my way down the steps into the basement of the Dwight R. Herbert Building at EIT. Herbert houses part of EIT's sciences department, with the other part being held in Jasper Hall next door. It's Perry's first week at his new job and I thought I could pay him a visit to brighten up his morning. Plus, it'll actually give me something to do instead of lay around the apartment. Cheering up a friend sounds better than more daytime television. And he *could* use some cheering up.

Like Rachel, he's still mourning the loss of his old lab, as well as the people who visited it. The events of what happened three weeks ago at Ellsworth Science and Technology Research—or ESTR as we called it—still haunt us, even with the change in setting. It's something I'm sure none of us will truly be able to escape.

At the bottom of the stairs in Herbert, I step into a crowded basement lounge. It's usually teeming with students who've

Chapter One

discovered this usually quiet solitude as a place to study. Today, though, the chatter grows with a mix of students and faculty alike.

Perry's lab is to the left, but through the crowd I spot my friend seated at one of the plush chairs in the corner, scrolling through his phone among several other men and women dressed in lab coats, ties, and other professional attire. Clearly, they're not students.

I make my way through the crowd and hand him his coffee. "What are you doing out here?"

He's startled when he first sees me, but smiles when he takes his cup. "Thanks."

It's still hard to get used to seeing Perry in professional clothing. Back at ESTR he usually wore T-shirts and jeans. Today, he's wearing black pants and a light blue dress shirt that sits tight against his belly. Consequences of having a desk job. And the fast food doesn't help, either. His white lab coat usually helps to hide that, but he's not wearing it right now. Still, it's such a difference from what I'm wearing. A black V-neck T-shirt that's tucked into my khaki shorts. Old habits die hard, apparently.

"What's going on?" I ask.

He motions to the group sitting around him. "We're all just waiting until we're given the go-ahead to go back in."

I scrunch my brow. "What do you mean?"

He points over to his lab. Turning, I see police tape stretched across the hallway with an officer standing guard outside it. Several other officers move about beyond the tape.

"Word has it someone was found dead in the lab this morning," he tells me.

My head snaps to him. "Who?"

He shrugs. "No idea. Naturally, they won't tell us anything."

I study the officers working behind the tape. There's an older man with wispy gray hair taking pictures just inside the doorway to Perry's lab. Behind him, a woman—judging by her plainclothes, I'm guessing she's a detective—murmurs quietly to two men in uniforms. She's wearing a gray pantsuit and her dirty blonde hair is pulled back out of her eyes.

"That's a shame," I say to my friend. "And at the start of the new semester, too."

"What a way to start off the school year," he adds.

"Any idea when you will be able to get back in?"

He shrugs again. "They keep saying they're almost done." He checks the time on his phone. "I've been here an hour so far." He points to one of his coworkers. Barry Murphy is a bald man with a red bushy beard that makes up for what he's lacking on the top of his head. I've met him once before. "Barry says they were here at six when he got here."

"What do you think happened?"

"Not sure, but since they're taking so long, I'm guessing they're suspecting foul play," he says.

"Who found the body?"

"Well, Barry was the first one here," Perry says. "But I haven't heard anything for sure. He would be my guess, though. The police said they want to talk to him."

"They probably want to talk to all of you since you all work out of the lab."

"True."

Clicking heels on the stairs turns both of our attention to another blonde woman descending with a cup of coffee in her hand. She smiles when we meet eyes and comes right to me.

"Hey! How are you?" She leans in and gives me a quick hug.

I smile awkwardly as I try to place where I know her from. She's definitely someone I've met since waking up in the cave.

"It's Lisa," she says. "We met at Vernon's dinner party."

"Oh, right!" Now I recognize her. She sat next to me at dinner with Marge, another one of Vernon's coworkers. "How have you been?"

"I'm doing okay," she says with a polite head nod. "I heard

about Vernon. It's so sad."

"Yeah, it really is," I say. "Any idea how his wife and kids are doing?"

She shakes her head. "I don't know, I was going to ask you the same thing. I haven't talked to them since the funeral."

"Me neither. I hope they're doing all right."

"Me too," she says. "So what have you been up to?"

Well, in the last three weeks I've been avoiding the subject of Arlus Cain somehow being my brother and focusing my energy on stopping fights and keeping track of the crime in the city, which hasn't been too terrible.

I keep all that to myself, though.

Hooking a thumb over my shoulder, I say, "Right now I'm just visiting Perry."

He nods a hello and comes around to my side.

"Oh, I'm sorry," she tells him. "I didn't see you there."

"Perry just started working here this week," I explain.

He motions to his lab. "It's now currently a crime scene, so that can't be a good omen."

Lisa ignores his quip. "Oh yeah, isn't that horrible? He was young, too."

"He was?" I ask.

She nods. "Yeah, when I got in this morning, the police hadn't quite closed off the area so I got a glimpse. He was just lying there."

"Blood?" I ask. "Was he stabbed or something?"

She shakes her head. "No blood as far as I could see, but I didn't get a real good look. They asked me to step out while they investigated. I had to answer all kinds of questions, just so they could rule me out as a suspect."

"I thought you worked at River Valley Holdings?" I take a sip of my coffee. "Isn't that how you knew Vernon?"

"I did—it was," she says. "Actually, right after Vernon's dinner party I accepted the job here."

"Doing what?" Perry asks.

"I'm the secretary for Dr. Henry Isaacs," she says. "It's similar to what I was doing at River Valley, but with a lot less stress. Plus, it's closer to home for me. I've actually been walking here every day so far."

"Oh wow, that is close," I say.

"Yeah." She cradles her cup between two hands. "So I take it you're not staying with the Michaels' anymore?"

I shake my head. "No, I've actually been staying with Perry for a while."

She glances over at him and then back to me. "Oh, I didn't realize you two were that close."

"Yeah, me, him, and Rachel kind of hit it off right away," Perry says.

"That's good." She turns to me. "Are you still taking classes here?"

"No, I'm not." Best to keep things short and as honest as I can.

"Are you working anywhere, then?"

Perry snorts beside me.

I shoot him a look and then turn back to Lisa. "Uh, no. I'm… I'm kind of in between jobs right now." At least I assume I had a job before I ended up in the cave. Either way, my best self is not coming through right now. I look like a pathetic mooch, which I guess I kind of am.

"Oh."

One word carries so much weight.

"He's looking," Perry tells her. "If you know of anything, let him know."

I smile. "Yeah, definitely."

Not sure what exactly I'm qualified for or how it's going to fit in with my Heat stuff, but it wouldn't hurt to have a job. That way I could help pay my way with rent and food and stuff at Perry's. It certainly wouldn't cover everything he does for me, but it would help.

She waves her finger and raises her eyebrows. "Actually, I might know of something."

"You do?" Perry and I say simultaneously.

She laughs. "Yeah. Ash, why don't you and I take a walk and we can talk about it?"

"Now?"

She motions to the police officers. "It's not like I'll be getting back in my office anytime soon."

"Very true." I turn to Perry. "I'll see you later."

"Hopefully I can get back to work sooner than later," he says. "Good luck."

"Thanks!"

Lisa and I head out to the courtyard just outside the Main Hall that centers the campus. It's a nice early-September day with clear skies and a gentle refreshing breeze. We pass groups of students buzzing with the excitement of returning to school and their friends. I can't help but note the stark difference between out here and the basement of Herbert.

We walk slowly, working our way around the courtyard. Neither of us say anything as we take in the change of scenery, feeling the warm rays on our skin.

"It's beautiful," she muses.

"Yeah," I murmur. Despite what she's saying being true, I can't get my mind off of the body in the basement. Who is it and what happened to them? And if it is foul play, who would do that to them?

"Makes me want to play hooky," she adds. "Especially since I can't get in my office, but this little break is nice."

"Hopefully the police will have answers soon," I tell her. "So you say you saw the body this morning?"

Lisa doesn't answer right away. Instead, she looks down and studies her feet, forgetting the bright sun while she ponders my question.

"I know how it sounds," she finally says. "But there were people in the lab already. Faculty who had already contacted the police and were just guarding the room before the police showed up. I didn't—"

I shake my head. "No, that's not what I'm suggesting."

Whoops, wrong way to start an interview. Even for an informal one, dead bodies are never an icebreaker.

"What do you do to relax?" I ask, trying to change the subject.

"What do you mean?"

"Well, after a long day at work, do you kick back with a glass of wine and a book? Go out with friends? Stay home and get a jump on laundry?"

Lisa gives me an odd look, but answers regardless. Must be she knows what I was looking for: an alibi. "I'm usually helping my daughters with their homework. Last night especially we were working on it until about eight o'clock. I watched some TV with my husband for a bit and then went to bed."

Nodding with a smile, I try not to make my brief questioning so awkward. "Any good shows?"

"I'm way behind on all the popular ones," she replies. "So my answer would be about three years old."

I laugh it off. Even if she did answer, I wouldn't know whether the show was new or old. With as much TV as I've watched in the last few weeks, none of it has triggered any sort of memory. Everything's new to me.

She lets out a deep breath. "Anyway, you're probably wondering what job I had in mind for you."

I grin, but don't offer a response.

"First, though," she goes on, "I'd like to get to know you a little better."

"Okay…"

"What kind of job experience do you have?" she asks.

Jumping right in with the tough questions. Then again, with

my unclear past, *most* questions are tough questions.

"Uh…not much, really," I reply. "I've been so focused on school and now that I'm not in school, it's…weird."

Lisa nods. "I get it. I was the same way in college. Too busy keeping my grades up that I didn't really map out what exactly I wanted to do *after* college." She shrugs. "Everyone's gotta start somewhere and where you start might not even be where you end up."

"That's true." I honestly haven't given much thought to my future. Too consumed with my past.

"Do you have any kind of passion for science?" she asks.

Does learning about my own unique abilities count?

"Passion? Uh…not quite," I tell her.

We both laugh.

"I have an interest," I continue. "I mean, my eyes don't *completely* glaze over when Perry and Rachel talk about work."

She chuckles. "Well, that's good. What I had in mind was a position at my office. With Dr. Isaacs."

"What kind of position?"

"Uh…maybe *position* isn't the right word," she clarifies. "Dr. Isaacs is a very efficient person—especially when it comes to his research. And you didn't hear this from me, but the only reason he's even teaching is so that he can have a designated lab here at EIT to work on that research."

"I certainly don't think I'm qualified to pick up the slack from his classes."

"No, of course not," she says. "He has a TA for that. What I had in mind—and I'll need to run this by Dr. Isaacs as well—is having you be a sort of lab assistant. I'm thinking you'd come in, clean up from the previous day's work—cleaning beakers, wiping tabletops, *disinfecting*, that sort of thing. Then once that's done, you can get the essential materials together for that day's work. Oh, and you would probably also be the best person to let me know about inventory levels and stuff like that because it's hard for me to keep track of that with everything else I need to do."

We turn around the edge of the courtyard and head back toward the Main Hall.

"So you're essentially just looking for someone to do the scut work," I simplify.

"Well yeah, but it'll be an essential part of the process—especially with Dr. Isaacs."

"If you say so."

"Just think about it," she says. "It'll probably only be minimum wage, part-time. And Dr. Isaacs usually teaches in the mornings, so if you could come in at like, eight, and leave by noon, that would probably be the best scenario. He's not really a fan of distractions. Sometimes even my typing on the computer gets on his nerves." She shrugs. "It's just the way he likes to work."

I nod and look down at my feet as we walk. "Okay. Um…the only issue I have is that I, uh, am kind of…*off the grid*, I guess you could say."

The delicate way of saying that I don't have any important government documents that prove I am who I am. At least, not in my possession. I'm sure Arlus would be able to tell me where those are. I'm sure Arlus could tell me a lot of things.

"What do you mean by 'off the grid'?" she asks.

"Well, I don't use a bank…or a car," I say. "So I don't have a driver's license or anything."

"You don't have a license?"

I shrug. "I've been doing fine with the bus." Lately, I've been walking most places or hitching a ride with Perry or Rachel. Or even flying as Heat.

"And you don't belong to any bank or anything?"

I shake my head. "Haven't had the need for one, honestly." I wonder if I have an account somewhere with a whole stash of money in it.

"All right, well…um, I could see if he'd be willing to pay

you under the table," she says. "It would depend, because I don't think we have the budget for the school to be paying you. It would have to come out of Dr. Isaacs' own pocket and I'm not sure he's even open to this whole position."

"Oh, this wasn't his idea?"

She shakes her head. "No, I just thought of it when you said you didn't have a job. But I'll talk to him about it. I just thought I'd pitch it to you first to see if you're even interested."

"No, that makes sense. I'm definitely interested. Sounds like an easy part-time job to keep me busy."

"Exactly. I think it'd be a perfect fit."

"Hopefully Dr. Isaacs does too," I say.

"I'm sure it'll be fine. Can I get your number so I can give you a call when I talk to Dr. Isaacs?"

I pull my phone out of my back pocket—something Perry got for me because he was too tired of me being unavailable all the time.

I read her my number and then add hers to my phone. Thankfully, she doesn't question why I have a phone, even though I don't use a bank or even have a license. Guess it's because cell phones are so commonplace.

"All right," she says when she's done taking my number. "I'll talk to him—er."

"What is it?"

"Well, I would say I'll see him later, but with the police in the lab, there's no telling when I'll see him. I'll be in touch as soon as I can, though."

"Sounds goo—"

Piercing screams ring out from one of the open windows in the Main Hall. Lisa and I have just made it back to the sidewalk in front of the stairs that lead up to the large front doors, so we hear everything clearly. Not that a scream that loud is hard to miss.

Racing up the stairs, I pull open the heavy wooden door and

follow the sound to a girl with dark curly hair standing at the top of the eastern staircase. She's crying, covering her mouth as her shoulders shake with sobs. Lisa comes up right behind me.

"What's going on?" I ask the girl.

"What's the matter?" Lisa gently touches the girl's shoulders.

I follow the girl's gaze down to the landing at the bottom of the stairs. Among a backpack, errant papers, and what appears to be sand or dirt, another girl lies lifeless.

Chapter Two

Lisa turns the curly-haired girl so she's no longer staring at the scene on the landing.

"You're okay." She wraps her arms around her. "Shh. You're okay."

I pull out my phone and am about to dial 9-1-1, but someone runs down the hall and says, "I called the officers from Herbert! They're on their way!"

Looking over, I study the body. She has long curly red hair, similar to her friend's. She's sprawled out on the floor, her backpack tossed near her feet with some books spilling out. Almost as if she tossed the bag when she fell backward. A folder lays open beside her, its contents scattered all over the landing among two textbooks. Looks like they're syllabi and other coursework papers. Nothing containing sensitive information from what I can tell. I can't spot any blood, but it doesn't mean it's not there. What's most obvious—and curious—is the dusting of sand everywhere, especially in the corners and along the stairs.

Dust Storm

Two people wind up dead only twelve hours apart? There's no way this is a coincidence. Who would want them dead? Why? How? The girl here on the landing looks like she was just walking to class. Well, except for the sand. That's really puzzling. Surely, this girl was not carrying a sack of sand in her backpack.

We only have a few precious moments before the police pull her away for their questioning. If these deaths are connected—and my gut is telling me they are—then I need honest, unbiased, initial reactions from this girl. I can't help anyone find out what happened if I don't know anything myself.

I step over to Lisa and the brunette with the curls. "What's your name?"

"This is Sarah," Lisa says for her. She holds her in an embrace and whispers to me, "She's really upset."

A warning that I need to tread carefully.

Gently, I place my hand on Sarah's shoulder. "Do you know who that is?"

She nods and sniffles, answering between sobs. "My—friend—Abby."

No wonder she's so upset.

"Did you see what happened?"

She shakes her head. "We were just talking and then—oh, my gosh, Abby!"

Lisa pulls her in tighter again for comfort.

"Sarah, focus," I say kind of harshly. "Did you see anyone or hear Abby say anything before it happened?"

"Ash, I'm sure the police will ask her all of this," Lisa interjects.

"I know, but if there's anything she might remember, we could—"

"Let it go, Ash." She challenges me with her eyes.

I step away and look down at the body again. It's obvious I'm not going to get very much out of Sarah right now. Better to take in what I can before the police section off the scene. The problem is, there's not a lot to see without being too obvious. We're already starting to attract a crowd. So far, everyone is keeping their distance, but if I approach Abby, soon everyone else will rush to her too. Best to take it all in from a distance. But without getting too close, there's not much more I can see from this vantage point.

Trying another tactic, I focus on how she might've been attacked. Obviously, she was carrying the folder and the books, but if her arms were full with that, chances are she wasn't carrying her backpack in her hands. So why was it tossed in the corner?

Turning back to Sarah, I ask, "Did Abby have her bag on her back?"

"What?" She looks at me with wet eyes.

"Her backpack. Was it actually on her back?"

She furrows her brow. "Um…I don't think so. Why?"

"Just wondering." I look back down the staircase. Did she drop them there to fend off her attacker? From the little Sarah told me, it doesn't sound like there was much of a fight.

As the crowd around us at the top of the stairs grows, so does a smaller one at the bottom of the stairs. Soon, police officers rush in through the crowd at the bottom—likely coming from the tunnels that connect the different campus buildings—and start pushing back the swarms of people. One officer tapes off the area while two officials—the man and the woman in plainclothes I saw in the basement of Herbert—duck under the tape and study the body.

"Can you all please take a step back?" the officer taping off the scene asks after he's ascended the stairs.

His voice pulls me back into reality and I move away from the steps a few feet.

"This is Sarah," Lisa tells him. "She was with Abby when she fell."

He nods. "We'll need to talk to her. Don't go anywhere."

The man and woman in sports coats come up the stairs and

approach Lisa and Sarah. Now that I see them up close, I notice that the man has a full head of black hair and a beard to match. Also, I can see how the woman's hair is threatening to fall out from her hair tie. Instead of fixing it, she simply tucks the few strands that have already escaped behind her ears.

"Sarah?" the man says. "I'm Detective Walter Watkins and this is my partner Detective Jenna Harkness. We need to ask you a few questions privately, if you don't mind."

"It's okay," Lisa tells her. "I'll be waiting right here."

"Actually, ma'am, if you and uh…" Harkness motions to me.

"Ash," I reply, holding back from saying my last name in case anyone recognizes it. The last thing I need is to be tied to Arlus Cain until I have a better handle on who I am. Besides, if I'm a missing person my name might ring a bell with the police. And they're not here to discuss me.

"Ash." She looks me right in the eyes, likely aware that I'm hiding something. "If you were all the first ones at the scene, we'll need to talk to each of you separately as well."

Noting the officers moving about down on the landing, I nod to Lisa. "You go ahead and take care of Sarah when she's done. I'll be fine."

"Okay."

Harkness moves her aside to a more private area while Watkins is deep in conversation with Sarah in their own corner of privacy. The girl looks scared—devastated—but she puts on a brave face to tell the detective what she saw. Apparently, the shock of Abby's death has faded enough for her to finish a complete sentence.

Facing the growing crowd around the hallway, I lean against the pony wall separating this floor from the emptiness above the bottom staircase, facing away from the commotion on the stairs. Hopefully it's not too obvious that I'm eavesdropping. As I strain to listen, I study the terrazzo floors, tracing the lines separating the different colors.

CHAPTER TWO

"…still waiting on the medical examiner," one of them says. "He should be here anytime now."

"It's pretty obvious, though," the second one says. "She slipped, must've clonked her head, and died."

I'm not buying it. The sand tells me it's not that simple.

"Don't be so sure," the first one scolds. "Look around. There's no blood."

"True, there's only sand. Same as there was in the next building. What do you think that's about?"

Well, that's something. Sand around one dead body is weird. Sand around two bodies—killed within twelve hours of each other—is a pattern.

"You think they're related?" he asks the first one.

"Could be. That's up to the detectives to figure out. There aren't any cameras in the stairwell here."

"There wasn't a good shot of that lab, either," the other one says.

"Exactly. Coincidence or planned attack? Hard to say."

Hmm. It's awfully convenient that both deaths happened where there weren't cameras. Now that there are two victims, I'm curious to find out what really happened. The sand suggests that it has to do with my kind of strange, but I need to be sure before I go digging around into things that the police are presumably going to uncover themselves.

"Mr…Ash."

I'm snapped out of my head as Harkness calls my name.

"Yes, ma'am?"

"Please call me Detective Harkness. 'Ma'am' would be referring to my mother."

"Sorry."

"Are you ready to answer a few questions?" She looks me up and down with a hard gaze, likely trying to gauge whether I'm a suspect.

"Uh…sure." I peer over her shoulder in an effort to spot Lisa and Sarah, but I can't make them out in the thinning crowd. I was hoping to get a chance to talk to Sarah some more. "Where did my friend go?"

"They finished up already." She looks down at her notepad. "Miss Sanders identified the victim as Abby Adams. Do you know that name?"

"No, I was just walking with a friend when we heard screaming and ran in." I turn and try to spot Lisa and Sarah out the window but it's no luck.

"Mrs. Lacell?"

"Who?"

"Lisa Lacell. The woman who was comforting Miss Sanders."

"Oh, I was talking to her, yeah."

"Are you a student here?"

I shake my head. "No, I'm—I was visiting a friend."

"Mrs. Lacell?"

"No, someone else."

She hooks an eyebrow. "And who is *that* friend?"

I clear my throat, feeling the weight of her scrutiny like a physical force. "Perry Griswold. He works in Herbert."

Both of her eyebrows go up now. "What room?"

"Uh…B120, I think."

She lets out a deep breath. "So the room that was the center of another police investigation this morning?"

"Uh…yeah, I guess."

Harkness eyes me. "What's your last name, sir?"

"It's, uh…Cain, ma'am—er, Detective." So much for keeping that bit of information to myself. I guess they probably would've eventually asked me for my name and information anyway, though.

"You seem nervous." She scribbles in her notepad.

I shrug and try my best to act casual. "I've never been interviewed by police before."

She studies me again. I can't tell if she believes me or simply lets my answer pass. Either way, I'm relieved when she turns her questions back to the body.

"So you have no connection to Miss Sanders or Miss Adams?"

"No."

"Can you describe the scene when you arrived?" she asks. "What was happening when you approached?"

"Not much, really," I start. "Lisa and I were walking by outside, heard Sarah—Miss Sanders—screaming, so we both ran in. When we got here, Sarah was standing at the top of the stairs in tears, looking down at Abby on the floor. Shortly after that, people started coming in to see what was going on."

"You didn't try to revive Miss Adams?"

I shake my head. "No. I guess I should've but…I don't know. I was just in shock from everything. I didn't notice her breathing and the sand left me really confused."

"Did Miss Sanders say anything when you arrived?"

"Just said that the girl—the victim—was her friend Abby and that they were 'just talking.'" I shrug. "I know something else happened because you don't die from talking, but I really don't think Sarah had anything to do with it."

She closes her notepad. "We hope not. Can I have your contact information in case I need to get ahold of you for further questions?"

After relaying the information and stealing one last glimpse of Abby—who is being lifted into a body bag by the medical examiner—I make my way back out to the sidewalk where Lisa and I were when we heard Sarah's screams. Back into the sunshine, away from the horrors inside these old campus buildings.

Searching up and down the sidewalk, I can't spot Lisa or Sarah anywhere. They must've already made it inside somewhere. Good for Sarah, but bad for me finding out more information. I need to talk to her while things are still fresh in her mind. Before the police pester her with more questions. My gut is telling me that this is the work of another super. If that's the case, the police won't be able to handle this on their own.

My plan to talk to Sarah having been avoided, I pull out my phone and text Perry.

"See what you can find out about the body in your lab. From co-workers, cops, whomever. A girl in the Main Hall was just killed in the same way."

A moment later, he texts back.

"I'll see what I can do. Where did you hear about the girl?"

"Lisa and I were the first ones there after it happened," I reply. "I'll explain later."

I slide my phone in my back pocket and consider my next option. I could go down to the basement and try to get information out of Perry's co-workers with him, but that would seem too forced. It's still his first week. They barely know him, let alone his friend. Why would they share stories with a complete stranger about something so sensitive? Better to let him naturally ask for the scoop in casual conversation. Besides, they might not even know anything more than I do anyway.

The most I can do right now is wait. To hear what Perry finds out and for an opportunity to talk to Sarah. If she told Lisa anything else, Perry might hear about it when Lisa returns to Herbert. If she doesn't tell him anything, I still have the job offer in my back pocket as an excuse to talk to her. I just need to be patient. And I'm discovering that that's not really my strong suit.

Back in the courtyard, I wander along a path under the tree canopy that blocks the day's sun. It's all I can do to not head back into the Main Hall or Herbert. I should probably get off campus to reduce the temptation to be nosy, but I want to be close in case something else happens. With two dead already, there's a good chance a third is on the way. I just wish I had more information to stop it from happening.

Halfway through the courtyard, something else catches my eye. Nothing specific, really, but the atmosphere of the place. The

Chapter Two

way the sun streams through the leaves on the branches above. The plush green grass. The crisp late-summer air. It's like it's begging to be made the most of.

What strikes me, though, is how familiar this all feels. Like I've been here before. Like I belong here.

Turning, I search for a place to sit and am immediately struck with a memory—both a genuine memory and a recollection of one of my flashbacks. The one of me and my girlfriend lying under a tree—*this* tree right in front of me.

The conversation comes back to me vividly. We were talking about our future. Lying together like we belonged here. Maybe we do. Maybe *I* do.

Spinning around, I search the faces of the students lying around the courtyard. I don't recognize any of them. More importantly, nobody recognizes *me*. If this is really where I belong, then surely *someone* would've noticed.

Still, I can't get the image of the girl from my vision out of my head. The questions burn inside me: could my girlfriend be walking around this campus, completely oblivious that I'm here? Is there a chance that I could bump into her and finally have a connection to the person I was before?

Chapter Three

Hey," Rachel says into the phone a few minutes later.

"Are you busy?" I ask.

"Just sat down for a quick lunch." A paper bag rustles on the other end. "What's up?"

"I take it you haven't heard the news." I'm sitting under the tree in the courtyard waiting. Whether that's for my girlfriend or Sarah depends on who I spot first. I really wish I knew the name of the girl from my visions.

"No, what happened?" Rachel asks with a mouthful.

"Well, EIT is the scene of two murders now."

"What!?" she shouts, then breaks into a short coughing fit. I can hear her tapping at her chest and the plastic cap of her water bottle hits the desk. Must be she's reaching for a drink.

"You okay over there?"

She coughs a few more times. "Went down the wrong pipe."

"Is that the technical term?"

"Focus, Ash. When did this all happen?"

Chapter Three

"Today. Someone found the first body in Perry's lab—"

"Is he okay?"

I glance up toward the Herbert building. The leaves on the twisted branches of the trees obstruct my view. "He's fine, yeah. I'm surprised he hasn't told you himself." I pick at the bark on the branch to my right and scan the sidewalks for any new students. It's quiet so it must be during a popular class time.

"Perry and I haven't been catching up as much as we used to," she admits. "At least now that we don't work together anymore. But you said he's okay?"

"Yeah, he's not the one who found the body. He just wasn't allowed into his lab."

The sound of more plastic carries from the other end as she reaches for the next thing in her lunch. "That's good."

"Yeah."

I pause, watching the group of kids twenty feet away in the grass. They're all laughing and talking. Enjoying being with each other. Like I used to do with Rachel and Perry at ESTR. We're still close, but it's not the same. Not like when we all had a reason to be under one roof every day.

"We should all hang out again soon," I tell her.

Papers shuffle on the other end, sliding until they splash on the floor in a paper avalanche.

"Dammit," she mutters to herself. "I'm sorry, Ash, what were you saying?"

"I want to see you guys again. All three of us. It's been a while."

"We've just been really busy."

And by "we," she means her and Evan.

"Plus," she goes on, "until recently, I've been unemployed."

I cringe. "Sorry."

"It's not your fault, Ash." Papers swish on her end as she picks up her mess.

"I know, but I still feel bad."

"It's just the way things are."

"Yeah. It sucks not having ESTR to be together and it's been making things a little more difficult for Heat stuff."

In the last three weeks, I've successfully prevented several crimes as Heat. Nothing as big as two murders. Typically just the usual robberies and assaults. Still, doing all of that felt like I was riding solo. Perry finally invented a communication device that could withstand the extreme fluctuations of my body temperature, but without knowing for sure if there's going to be someone on the other end, it's not much help.

Perry and Rachel are busy working. With other people. They can't just sign off in the middle of the day to walk me through my trips as Heat. Not anymore, at least. It's the sacrifice I've had to make now that ESTR is gone.

"You've done okay, though," Rachel says. "Besides, I don't think either of us consider our current jobs permanent. I'm not enjoying sharing an office with everyone—especially when they can't even use the organization system I came up with! Seriously, how hard is it to put—" Plastic clangs on the other end. "—the pens away!"

"Actually, Perry has it pretty good where he is," I admit. "He seems to like what he's doing and he says he's paid more than he was before, too. Plus, his coworkers all seem nice."

"Oh."

"Sorry." Glancing up, I note a professor stepping out of the cafeteria with a cup of coffee and following the sidewalk along the edge of the courtyard.

"It's not your fault," Rachel repeats.

When ESTR went under, Perry was able to find a job relatively quickly—a job that's actually more in line with what he's always wanted to do in terms of the work: build tech. Rachel, however, hasn't been as lucky. Despite all her talents and previous successes, she hasn't been able to find a job doing what she loves: research. Instead, she landed a job as a lab technician at Ellsworth General Hospital downtown, which comes with a steep pay cut and odd hours. The result of finding work in a competitive field.

"How's your job?" I ask. "Any better?"

She sighs. "It's not that it's a bad job. The work's okay. Not my favorite, but I know what I'm doing. And the people are okay, I guess. But…"

"But it's not your own lab with your own hours and your own research."

"Yeah."

"I get it. It was a big, unexpected shift. You'll find something better eventually."

"Maybe not."

"Don't say that."

"Well, I just feel stuck that this was the only thing I could find that would actually help me pay my mortgage. Too bad it doesn't help me pay for much else."

"Keep looking," I say encouragingly. "Something better is bound to turn up."

"Yeah," she says with a sigh. "Anyway, I'm sure you didn't call to hear me complain about work."

"Well no, but I don't mind chatting."

She grunts a laugh. "I'm not chatting. I'm whining. What else did you want to know?"

"Well…I was hoping that you would be able to tell me what would make someone spontaneously die."

There's a pause and then she asks, "This is about those bodies found, isn't it?"

"Just answer the question."

"You answer mine first!"

I let out a deep breath. "Okay fine. It is about the bodies—"

"Ash, you really shouldn't be sticking your nose where it doesn't belong," she scolds. "Burglars for petty larceny is one thing, but *murder* is something else entirely."

"I know, but—"

"Did you contact the police?"

"They were already there, yeah. I just—"

"Then let them do their job."

"Rachel, I can't ignore this!" I blurt before she can cut me off again.

"I get that, but you've already got enough on your hands, like the Gatekeeper. He hasn't shown up anywhere since ESTR burned down and it's not sitting well with me."

"Maybe he's dead." I don't believe my own words.

"I don't think so and neither do you. It's better not to get involved with anything else because he'll probably show up again."

"Yeah," I say as a sigh. There's no denying the fact that she's right. "But whether it's petty larceny or murder, a bad thing is still a bad thing. I can't just ignore that. It's not like I have any other sense of purpose in life. So let me do what I can to help."

Her end of the phone is quiet for a few seconds. Finally, she says, "I guess you've got a point."

"So is there something, medically speaking, that can make adults go from seemingly healthy to dead on the floor?"

She sighs and pauses again. "Not really. Well, not spontaneously. Someone might *appear* healthy, but what's really happening is that there are undetected symptoms of greater issues occurring somewhere in their bodies. How old were the victims?"

"Well, I don't know about the first one, but the girl was a teenager. Her friend looked young. Maybe even a freshman."

"Okay, so like eighteen?"

"Yeah, that's probably right."

"Well, there's SADS, which happens to adolescences and young adults—"

"What's SADS?"

"*Sudden arrhythmic death syndrome,*" she explains. "It's rare and it's usually caused by undetected heart disease or mixing medication or some other deformity of the heart. Of course, it usually only occurs when a person is sleeping. Neither of these deaths were in a dorm room or somewhere where they might've been lying down or taking a nap, were they?"

"No. Like I said, the one was found in Perry's lab and the other was walking and talking to her friend just before she collapsed." Or was attacked. I'm not convinced this was all innocent, but checking into spontaneous deaths is the easiest lead right now.

"Hmm. I'll have to look into it then."

"If that SADS thing is rare, what are the chances of two people dying of it on the same campus within a few hours of each other?"

"Equally rare," she muses. "But not completely out of the realm of possibility, I suppose. If you're really going to look into this, you'll need to cover all of your bases. Were there any other possible signs of death? Blood? Evidence a weapon was used?"

I smile, but don't acknowledge it. She's hooked now too. "No blood that I could see on the girl. I didn't get a good look at her and I didn't even see the first body, so I don't *think* there were any visible wounds. But I know for sure there were no weapons. Well…not the traditional kind."

"What do you mean?"

"There was sand all around both bodies."

"Sand?"

"Yeah, like from the beach, I guess."

"That's odd. I'm not an expert on weapons by any means, but I can't think of any that would discharge sand when launched. What would be the benefit? Or the cause?"

"I don't know, but like you said, I need to cover all of my bases."

"And be careful with that," she adds. "If you talk to people that the police have already talked to—or *before* the police get to them—things could get ugly."

"Yeah yeah yeah," I rattle off quickly.

"I'm serious, Ash."

"I know. I'll be careful. Is there anything else you could think of that might help me figure this out?"

"No, not related to that. But I was thinking about it, and until you remember who you are, it's probably best not to go out and meet *too* many people."

"Why's that?"

"What if someone recognizes you? You don't know what your past entails or if you have any enemies or standing warrants."

I roll my eyes. I might not know who I am exactly, but I'm pretty sure I'm not a criminal.

"And if someone *does* recognize you and you blow by them on the street, what will they say if they're someone important in your life?" she continues. "What if you don't even remember if they're your mother, brother, friend, girlfriend?"

"I remember her."

"Who?"

"My girlfriend."

"You do?"

"Yeah. Remember I said I had a vision about that girl I felt like I knew?" I pause, waiting for a response, but she doesn't offer one. "That girl is my girlfriend. Or was. Or something. I don't know."

"Did you have another vision about her?" Her voice is curious, but otherwise hollow.

"Not another one, but I remember more about her. Well, sort of. I stumbled on the place we were in the vision."

"Where was that? Uh…the tree, right?"

I nod and watch a couple take a seat against a tree about ten feet away. "Right."

"So where is it? Tell me more."

"Well, it's actually in the courtyard on campus," I say.

"At EIT?"

Chapter Three

"Yeah. There are a bunch of trees all over, but I recognized this one instantly. I'm actually sitting under it right now, hoping more memories are sparked or maybe even that I run into her."

"Oh." Her voice deflates further.

"That wasn't quite the reaction I was expecting."

"I—hmm—uh—I just don't want you to be disappointed if it doesn't turn out the way you expect it to."

"What do you mean?"

"Well, picture it from her side. You were her boyfriend—or *are*, maybe—and then you just disappear for six weeks, at least. That's how long you've been out of the cave for. She's probably worried sick about you and then suddenly you show up happy and healthy with no recollection of who you were before. It's suspicious and a little unbelievable—"

"But it's the truth!"

The couple glances my way, but return to their cuddle time. Gross.

Then again, that's basically what I remember from my vision, so I guess I can't throw stones.

"I know, Ash," Rachel says. "But she won't necessarily believe it's the truth. Besides, for all you know, a year has passed between that vision and now. Or more. Some of the other visions you've had were from your childhood. How do you know this girl is even still your girlfriend?"

My heart sinks as I realize how right she is. I can't expect everyone to be able to jump right back into my life with me. Especially when I don't even know what kind of life I lived before. And where would that leave this new life I'm creating? Would I still have time for Rachel and Perry and Heat if I had a family again?

My eyes wander across the courtyard. Through the trees, I spot a bouncing mass of dark curls. Sarah is heading toward the cafeteria. It's the perfect moment since most of the students are still in morning classes.

"Ash, I just want you to be prepared for all the possible outcomes," Rachel says in my ear.

"Huh? Oh yeah. I will. I am. I—I gotta go. Bye." I'm about to click off when she calls out again.

"Wait!"

I keep my eye on Sarah as she closes the distance to the brick building that houses the campus dining options. I'm not going to catch her in time. Not without running and that's a surefire way to scare her off.

"I think it's probably time that you do some research on yourself," Rachel says. "Now that Perry's at EIT—and you know you were, or are, a student there—maybe he can look in the student database to find you and help you remember what your major was—or is—and what some of your interests are. If that doesn't work, try the Ellsworth Public Library. They're bound to have high school yearbooks or something that'll help you remember something."

I'm only half listening. Instead, I watch the door that Sarah just disappeared into and wonder how much of a creep I would be if I went in there and followed her. After about half a second of deliberation, I determine that that would be crossing a serious line. I'm better off waiting for her to come out on her own before I approach her.

"Yeah, sounds great, Rach. But I really have to go now. Bye." Clicking off, I make my way over to a bench near the sidewalk leading to the cafeteria.

Hopefully Sarah doesn't take too long in there—or take another exit. Right now, she's my best lead in figuring out what happened to those victims. I'm willing to wait.

Chapter Four

Sarah doesn't notice me right away when she walks out of the cafeteria. She's carrying a plastic bag with a styrofoam box inside. Her eyes are locked firmly on the sidewalk in front of her, clearly lost in her own head.

I indulge in the creeper status a bit more when I step out from under the shade of the trees as she passes by.

"Sarah, hi—"

She jumps when she sees me and takes a careful step backward. Her eyes are puffy and red. "I don't want to talk anymore." Pushing by me, she marches on without waiting for a response from me.

"I just want to make sure you're okay." I follow behind her, keeping my distance so I don't appear too clingy. Or creepy.

"You want to talk about what I saw and I *don't* want to talk about it."

"Well yeah, but mostly I want to know how you're doing."

"It doesn't matter." She turns the corner and follows a different sidewalk back toward the dorms along Chestnut Avenue.

"What doesn't matter?" I ask.

"What I say."

"Why wouldn't it matter?" I counter. "You saw what you saw. There's no denying that."

Sarah reaches the door but stops and turns on me before she can swipe her card to enter. "Look, if even my parents doubt what I saw, then you're not going to believe me either."

I stare at her as she holds my gaze. "She didn't fall, did she?"

Her red eyes narrow as she studies me, likely trying to determine what I know. Finally, she asks, "What?"

"Your friend Abby. A fall isn't what killed her."

She swallows hard. "That's what the police are saying—"

"I want to know what you're saying."

Another pause. She looks at her feet. "I don't know for sure, but…"

I nod over to the nearest bench along the sidewalk. "Do you mind telling me what you saw and what you think really happened?"

She glares at me again, unmoving. "This isn't some kind of trick, is it? You're not with a newspaper or something, are you?"

I put up my hands in surrender. "No media affiliation here. Just someone who wants to know what happened to a girl who was too young to die." I extend my hand. "I'm Ash."

She takes it and says, "Sarah, but you already knew that."

I smirk and lead her to the bench. "Why don't you start from the beginning? What were you guys doing in the Main Hall?"

"Going to the registrar's office to switch classes." Her voice already starts wavering. "We…changed it so that—" She sniffles. "So that we could have a class together."

I wish I came prepared with tissues or something. Instead, I reach over and rub her shoulder. Luckily, she's prepared and reaches in her plastic bag and pulls out the wad of napkins sitting on top of the styrofoam container.

Chapter Four

"Are you both freshmen?"

She nods. "She's a biology major—or was—and I'm psychology. We thought we could take some of our Gen Ed classes together, but that's not going to happen now." She blows her nose hard in the napkin.

"So what happened when you left the registrar's office?" I ask. "Where did you go from there?"

She shuts her eyes tight and her shoulders shake as the memory consumes her. It's so fresh that I feel bad pushing for more details like this, but a traumatic experience like this won't ever fade completely. It'll never be easy for her to talk about. And if I'm going to stop more students from dying, I need to move quickly, which requires answers.

After another minute, she gasps out her response. "That was just before—just before—" She sobs again and I rub her shoulder some more.

In an effort to help her—and myself—I try to coach out the rest of the story. The quicker I can get through this, the quicker she can be done with me. "Okay, so when you walked out of the office, did you head toward the staircase or stop somewhere else first?"

She wipes at her eyes. "We went to the staircase."

"How did you two get separated?"

She swallows hard again and points down to her backpack. "I stopped to fill up my bottle at the fountain."

In a mesh pocket on the side of her bag, I notice a black Tervis bottle. "And that's when it happened?"

She nods again. "It wasn't long that we were apart. Maybe fifteen seconds."

"Why didn't Abby wait for you?"

"She was anxious to get back to her dorm room to get started on homework."

Homework this early in the semester for a freshman? It's only the first week of classes.

"Okay, so you stopped to fill your bottle and Abby kept walking?"

"Yeah. The fountain is just around the corner from the staircase. Out of view, though. She always takes the stairs two at a time, but I don't think she tripped."

Thinking back to earlier when Lisa and I first ran in when Sarah screamed, I remember seeing a drinking fountain on the wall adjacent to the stairs. If Sarah was filling up her bottle, she couldn't have seen anything that happened around the corner on the stairs.

"So what do *you* think happened?"

Sarah shrugs. "She screamed and then she sounded like she was choking. When I came around the corner—" Her voice raises after each word until her sorrow leaves her unable to finish. Instead, she motions with her hand. Up, and then swiftly down.

"You saw her fall?"

Another nod. "I saw her *drop*."

"Like she was suspended in the air?"

"I don't know. Maybe." She shrugs. "That's impossible, though, right?"

Apparently impossible is subjective. "Did you see anyone else?"

She licks her lips and studies the ground.

"Sarah, did you see anyone else?" I repeat.

She takes a deep breath. "No. Not really. I was too focused on Abby. But…"

"But what?"

"I think I might've heard a door at the bottom of the stairs push open."

"Who?"

"I don't know. I just started screaming. I wasn't really paying attention."

From the quick tour of the campus Perry gave me, I remember walking down that same staircase and out the door at the end. It leads right to the underground tunnel system throughout campus. There's no telling where that person might've been running off to.

One thing's for sure, though. If Abby was screaming seconds before Sarah heard the door open and someone ran *away* from it, they're a suspect. I just need to find out *who* that is.

"Everything happened so fast," Sarah continues. "One second Abby and I were laughing and the next she was—"

I put up my hand to stop her. "I understand. Do you think someone choked her?"

I didn't get a good look at Abby's neck, but it's a possibility. Doesn't explain the sand, but it's a theory.

She shakes her head. "We weren't separated long enough."

"What about any heart conditions?" I ask, testing Rachel's theory. "Do you know if Abby had any abnormalities with her heart or was taking any medications for anything?"

Sarah furrows her brow and shakes her head. "No. Abby was healthy. As far as I know, she wasn't taking any pills or anything."

"Was there anyone who might've wanted to hurt her? Ex-boyfriends, former friends, that sort of thing?"

Leaning back, she looks at me with suspicious eyes. "I already told the police this. Are you sure you're just trying to make sure I'm okay? I think you're just being nosy."

"You're right, I crossed a line. I'm sorry." Pausing for a moment to recoup, I try a different tactic. "What about a boyfriend? Is there anyone you'd like me to contact so you don't have to relive this again?"

"No, she doesn't have a boyfriend," she says. "Well…not really."

"Not really?"

"I mean, he wasn't *technically* her boyfriend," she starts. "She denied it when I asked her about it."

"Who?"

"Mitch Mantel. We went to high school with him. Actually,

he and Abby were neighbors back home. He's a student here too. They've been—or they *were*—spending a lot of time together. All through senior year and throughout the summer." She shrugs. "I guess he'd probably want to know."

"So they weren't officially dating?"

She shakes her head. "Not according to Abby."

I nod. "Do you have his number? I'll give him a call and tell him the news."

"Yeah." She relays the information and then adds, "I think his room is in Frederick."

Craning my neck, I glance in the direction Sarah points and take in the stately building with intricate brickwork. Clearly, a campus original. Quite different from the boxy modern-style dorm building that Sarah calls home.

"So no exes?" I turn back to her.

"Just Jim."

"Last name?"

Another quizzical look, but she answers anyway. "Uh…Jerrick. But he's probably working."

"How long ago did they break up?"

"Maybe a few months. It was during senior year."

"When she was talking to Mitch?"

She rocks her head back and forth. "It was all about the same time. Her and Mitch started hanging out more after she broke up with Jim, but I don't think that's why they broke up."

"So why *did* they break up?"

"She wanted to go to college and he thought it was a waste. He was an asshole. Still is, probably."

"Sounds like it."

"He was very controlling," she goes on. "And very jealous. She lost all her guy friends because he didn't want her to have any—which is why he was pissed when she started hanging out with Mitch more. Breaking up with him was the best thing she ever did."

I nod. "Any idea where he works?"

"His dad's friend hired him as a mechanic apprentice or something."

"Do you know where?"

She shakes her head. "Don't know, don't care."

"Okay. I'll leave you alone with the questions." I flash a smile. "Thank you so much for talking with me. I'll get in touch with Mitch and let him know what happened. Let me give you my number if you want to talk."

She hands me a clean napkin and pulls out a pen from her backpack. "I don't know what I'm going to do without her."

"Take all the time you need." I hand her back the napkin with my phone number. "She was your best friend. Nobody expects you to bounce back easily from this."

———

THE PERSON AT the computer next to me snickers as I slowly peck the keyboard with my index fingers. This is the first time I've even stepped foot in the library—that I know of, at least. Using a computer, let alone *typing*, is not something that comes naturally to me. Judging by the way everyone else's hands hover above the keys, though, I'm clearly doing it wrong. But finger-tapping still gets the job done.

In Google's search bar, I finally finish typing out Jim Jerrick's name. Asking simple questions about Google resulted in more snickers and jeers from my computer neighbors. Meh, if it gets me the information I need, that's all that matters. My humiliation will subside. Abby's death will not.

I tried calling Mitch to get some answers out of him, but after several rings, his phone went to a recording: "This is Mitch, leave a message and I'll call you back."

I didn't bother leaving a message for him. He probably just didn't answer because he didn't recognize the number. I'll try again later. For now, I need to try to find a way to get in touch with Jim Jerrick.

Several results show up under his name. Links to Facebook, Whitepages, and an attorney sharing the same name in Seattle. I click the one for Facebook. Perry's made enough comments about it that I know what it is. The next page shows me a list of people from all over the world. I scroll through it until I find the person from Ellsworth and click on his page.

It doesn't show me much—Facebook prompts me several times to sign up to add him as a friend in order to see more. Yeah, that's not going to happen. What *is* listed on his page, though, is his place of employment: Paul's Auto. So original. Then again, if it's a family shop, I shouldn't expect an original name. Clicking through that link brings me to the auto shop's Facebook page, which lists an address. I copy it down and bring up the map I saw at the top of the Google page.

Finger-jabbing the keyboard again, I type in the address to show exactly where in the city it is. Easier than I could've ever imagined. Not too bad for someone who types like a woodpecker.

Closing out the browser, I get to my feet and head to the door. If I can corner Jim and ask him about Abby before the police get to him, I'll hopefully get more information out of him than if I question him after the fact. If Jim has something to hide and gets defensive about being questioned twice, I'd rather he get defensive with the police who have other means of getting him to talk.

I'm not naïve enough to think that they're not going to talk to him too. Always suspect the boyfriend or ex. Which reminds me...

Stopping halfway down the grand front steps of the library, I pull out my phone and call Mitch's phone again. It rings once, twice, three times before cutting to his recording again.

"Dammit," I murmur to myself. At least I have a way to get

in touch with Jerrick. Hopefully he doesn't catch wind that he looks like a suspect in his ex-girlfriend's murder. I'll just have to keep calling Mitch if I need another lead. If all else fails, I could ask around about him on campus, but that could lead to more problems.

Before I slip my phone back in my pocket, it buzzes with a text from Perry.

"I got the scoop from everyone at work who knew something," he writes. "Are you at the apartment?"

"No, I'm at the library." I step toward the bus station, but hesitate before I officially take my place among the queue of people waiting to get on.

Another buzz. "Oh, I got sent home early because the EPD was taking too long in my lab."

Well, that might mean that the death is a puzzle for them as well. Not that it's a surprise with the sand. That's still stumping me.

I wonder if they've made the connection to Jerrick yet and if they've talked to him. Should I head there now and try to get the jump on them? Or would that risk running into the police and having to explain why I'm there?

I decide to talk to Perry first. He might have something that would point to a better lead that the police may already be on. Any information I can get to piece this thing together myself—and stop the killer—is another step closer to preventing someone else's untimely death.

Tapping at my phone screen, I write back, "I'll be there soon."

Chapter Five

Perry leans on his crossed arms on the kitchen counter as I finish relaying everything that's happened today. From the chat with Lisa to my trip to the library, I dish it all out without any interruptions from him. I sit across the counter in one of the barstools and lean back once I'm finished.

"Wow, it's been a day for you, hasn't it?" he says.

I roll my eyes. "That's for sure."

"So I take it you're going to check out this Jim Jerrick guy?"

"That's where I was headed before you texted me. What did you find out from everyone at work?"

"Well, like the girl you found in the stairwell, the guy in the lab was also a student."

My eyebrows jump up. "Really?"

He nods. "Mm-hmm. He worked with the custodial staff as part of the work study program through his financial aid."

"He was a student…" I murmur to myself. That makes two of them. Even less of a coincidence. Who would be going after

44

students on campus?

"Yeah," he goes on, "and that explains why the police are taking so long in my lab."

I look up at him, confused. "Why's that?"

"He was a *student*, Ash. I can only imagine the school asked them to keep it quiet—especially when another student was found dead."

"Abby."

"Huh?"

"Her name was Abby. Let's call her that." It's the least I can do to give her the respect she deserves. If someone was ruthless enough to kill her in broad daylight and leave her on the floor, I can at least use her name instead of calling her "the body," "the girl," or "the victim."

"Oh okay. Anyway, with the new semester and the deadline for dropping classes still a week or two away, the school probably wants to keep these murders under wraps as much as possible. It wouldn't be good for its bottom line if a lot of students started withdrawing due to safety concerns."

"I can't blame the students, though," I say. "Or their parents. It has to be terrifying to think that you or your kid could be the next victim."

"I know."

"Although I hope EIT is more concerned about campus safety than tuition money."

Perry raises his hands and shrugs. "That's just my theory."

"What about the student in the lab? What's his name?"

He shakes his head. "I don't know. Barry said he didn't really get a good look at his face and the rest of us haven't been allowed inside yet."

"Then how do you know it was a he? And how do you even know he was a student?"

"It's what Barry told me," Perry says. "He said the janitors always stick the newbie students at the basement level."

"Hopefully that policy will change."

"I doubt it, but maybe. Anyway, nobody I talked to today knew his name. Everyone just figured he was new because he was on basement duty. But I did get a suspected cause of death."

My eyes grow large. "You did? How?"

"The police were interviewing everyone who worked in both of the labs they had closed off to rule out any suspects," he explains. "I was one of the last ones Detective Watkins interviewed and he let it slip that the cause of death for both victims was asphyxiation."

"From the sand?"

He shrugs. "He didn't elaborate because he realized right away that he messed up."

"So they're thinking it was murder?"

"That's what it sounds like."

Choking on sand. What a horrible way to die.

"Do you think it was someone at the school?" I ask.

"Probably," Perry says. "It was certainly someone who knew where that boy would be."

"You're sure it was a boy?" I ask. I don't want to proceed on hunches and guesses, but that's mostly what we've got right now.

"That's what everyone at the lab told me."

"Do you think it might be any of them?"

"No," he says quickly.

"Perry…"

"Ash, my coworkers didn't kill a student. This is still a new job, don't ruin it for me."

"You're right, it is a new job, which means that you don't *really* know your coworkers," I counter. "How do you know they're not secretly murderers? Or at least one of them."

He lets out a deep breath, no argument available.

"Do you know who found the body?"

"Not officially, but Barry is usually the first one in and the last one out."

"Interesting."

"He didn't kill him," Perry says.

"Maybe not, but it's something to think about. Do you think you can get into the school's database to try to figure out the first victim's name?" I push away Rachel's idea that Perry could also find out who I am too. Abby and the other student are more important right now.

He stares at me for a moment and then turns away. "Uh… no, I don't think I really have access to that. I don't work with students, other than a few in graduate programs. And even that's only minimal contact."

I catch his eye. "What aren't you telling me?"

"Rachel texted me today."

"Okay…"

"She's worried you're digging too deep into these deaths."

I roll my eyes and look away. "They're highly suspicious. *Murders*, Perry."

"Yeah, and the police will handle it. Why do you have to get involved?"

That throws me off. Perry has always been in support of me using my powers.

"Isn't it obvious? Students don't just drop dead out of nowhere," I say. "Besides, the sand at each crime scene suggests it might be someone like me."

"Like you?" he asks.

"With powers."

"How?"

"Rachel and I couldn't think of any weapon that would shoot—or discharge—sand when fired," I explain. "And that's not to mention the fact that from what I could tell with Abby, there was no sign of any weapon wound."

"That doesn't mean it's a super."

"Why else would there be sand by both bodies?"

He turns to the fridge and pulls out a tall can of iced tea. "I don't know. Maybe they're both geology students."

I shoot him a look when he turns back to me. "And they were carrying that much sand with them? At the *beginning* of the semester? Abby's friend said they were coming from the registrar office. And the student found in your lab wasn't even going to class. He was working. Besides, Abby's friend told me she was a biology major, *not* geology."

He shrugs. "I still think there's a more plausible explanation."

"And I think I have a responsibility to make sure that's the case," I counter. "Isn't this what you were pushing me to do when you made me the Heat suit? Fight the bad guys? That's what I'm doing now. I just need to help the good guys in the process. If a super is involved at all, the police aren't going to be able to handle that."

He grins and shakes his head. "You just had to use my own words against me, didn't you?"

I smirk. "Did it work?"

"Sort of. I know what I said and I know where you're coming from. I get it. I'm just worried you're getting too tangled up in this. And I'm sure that's Rachel's hesitation too. You jumped right into this case—and other cases—really quickly."

"Other cases?"

"Before this morning, how did you spend your days?"

I look away, knowing he used the same tactic I just did with him: throwing my own words and actions back at me. From armed robberies to grand theft auto, I've handled a lot in the last few weeks.

"Exactly," he says as if reading my mind. "Look, I'm not saying you shouldn't dig into this a bit, I'm just saying you need to tread carefully. After what happened with Vernon, which changed all of our lives, I don't think it's a bad thing to take things slow. And I think that's what Rachel's saying too."

I nod. "Okay. I get it."

"What about you? Have you done any digging into your past

now that you remember your girlfriend?"

I shake my head. "No, I haven't."

"Well, you should. What you remembered today is huge! It means you're likely a student at EIT. Maybe you can go to campus security and tell them you forgot your ID. That would give you your ID number that can get you into your own school records online."

"To what end?" I ask. "What would I find? My major? The classes I've taken? Whether I'm an A student or a B student? Stuff like that is not going to tell me who my family is."

"It would probably list your address and contact information too," he says. "That could put you in touch with—"

"No, Perry."

He sighs, but doesn't offer anything else for a while.

During the lull, I type out a text to Mitch's phone. "Hi Mitch. My name is Ash. I have some news about a friend of yours. Please call me ASAP." Hopefully that brief explanation will be enough for him to call me back. Hopefully that will also get me out of this conversation with Perry about my past.

After I send the text, Perry says, "I've been working on this idea I had about how you can get more from your flashbacks."

I narrow my eyes. "What do you mean?"

"I believe there's a way for me to develop a device that would actually let you live out your flashbacks."

"Like virtual reality?"

He rocks his head back and forth. "Almost. More like watching TV, but…strapped to your face."

"I'm not following."

"By tapping into key points in your brain, I should be able to develop a device that will project the images from your memory to a screen," he explains. "Rachel's been helping me a little bit with some of the more biological aspect of it, but she's not a neurologist. However, I have been working on a set of goggles that would allow you to see what your vision is once I figure out the biology part. For privacy."

I nod slowly. "So…like virtual reality."

He rolls his eyes. "Fine, that's what it is. Either way, hopefully it will make you aware of some of the more minor details you might be missing when you experience these visions."

"You really think you can create something like that?"

He takes a step back and motions to himself, as if he's a grand prize. "Have you met me? Of course I can."

Now it's my turn to roll my eyes.

"Seriously, though, you should really start looking into who you are," he pushes.

Getting up from the chair, I plop on the couch and spread my legs out across it. It's a small apartment, so it doesn't really do much to put space between us, but it still sends a message that I don't want to talk about this anymore.

Apparently, Perry ignores that message.

"Now that you know your last name and that Arlus is somehow your brother—which I guess is debatable because it's impossible—but it still gives you the tools you need to really discover who you are."

I study my fingers as I work the dirt from the tree bark out from under my nails. Lately I've been trying not to think too much about my past. Now that I've been out of the cave for almost six weeks without anyone from my past finding me, it's becoming more and more apparent that I don't have a big support system to return to. Maybe none at all. Arlus supposedly being my brother isn't helping. Nor is it a good sign.

"You're Ash Cain—"

I glare at him. "*Don't* call me that." The less I can associate myself with Arlus, the better.

He sighs and comes around the counter into the living room and takes a seat at the end of the couch by my feet. "Look, I know it's going to mean a big change, but you can't stay here forever. You have a family, Ash. You deserve to sleep on *their* couch."

He pauses and waits for a smile from me that doesn't come.

"Anyway, I get it if you're not ready," he continues. "I'll talk to Rachel and get her to try to back off a little, but the fact is: sooner or later you're going to have to figure out who you are. You can't hide from it."

We sit in silence for a while again. I wonder if he expects me to respond to his pep talk, but I don't. It's not that I don't appreciate it. I just simply don't want to think about it. Not with these murders at EIT. What about *their* families? Unlike me, Abby and that student in the basement aren't ever coming home. I'm just putting off *my* return home. And if I don't figure out who's killing students, there are going to be even more heartbroken families.

"Are you sure you can't try to hack into the student records?" I finally ask him.

"Uh…I could try, I guess. But hacking isn't really my forte," he says. "I could give it a shot, though."

"Good, thanks." I swing my legs around onto the floor and sit up.

"So does this mean you're ready to figure out who you are?"

My head snaps to him, brow furrowed. "What?"

Right, he wasn't following my train of thought.

"No, I meant for the victims," I clarify. "The girl who was found in the stairwell is Abby Adams. She's a freshman—or *was*. And I'm willing to bet that if the kid found in the lab was a newbie, he was a freshman too."

Perry gives me a disapproving look, but doesn't try to talk me out of it. "He could've just been a new work study student because his financial situation changed between semesters. Or maybe he just took a few years off before going to college. Or maybe he's a middle-aged college student who wanted to start a new career. There are a lot of theories."

Dust Storm

"It's a start." I get up and head toward the door. "Text me if you find anything."

"I probably won't check until tomorrow—where are you going?"

"I'm going to go talk to Abby's ex."

I'm out the door before I can hear any objections.

Chapter Six

Paul's Auto sits on the outskirts of town. Only two streets over from where the city line marks the start of the suburb of Sun Vista. The mechanic shop sits close to the street with two parked cars in the small front parking lot and another two on the street. Through the open garage doors, I can see there's a large parking lot behind the building, too.

Bent over the hood of a car in the shop, there's a man in denim coveralls with his arm buried deep in the engine. A red bandana wrapped around his head keeps the sweat out of his eyes and his dark hair out of his face.

I step forward into the garage, out of the hot sun, and clear my throat to get his attention.

He looks up and raises his eyebrows.

"Excuse me, I was hoping I could talk to Jim Jerrick." I put my hands in my pockets to try to act casual.

He stands up straight and reaches for a rag to wipe the grease off his hands. It's splattered all up his arms to his rolled up sleeves by his elbows. "That's me. Who're you?"

"I'm Ash," I say timidly. "I, uh, was hoping I could talk to you, um, about your old girlfriend Abby."

This isn't at all how I rehearsed it on the bus ride over here. I'm sputtering, letting my nerves get the better of me.

"What about her?" He reaches over to his toolbox and grabs something before returning back to the car. "I haven't seen her since we broke up."

"When exactly was that?"

"Last year. She got a little high and mighty as soon as she was accepted to that hoity-toity school across the river."

"So you didn't initiate the breakup?"

"No, I didn't."

"You haven't had any contact with her since?"

He looks at me again. "Who did you say you were with?"

"I didn't." I add quickly, "Where were you this morning?"

Jerrick narrows his eyes. "What difference does that make? Who are you? Why are you asking me all these questions? Are you another one of her boyfriends?"

"She had other boyfriends?"

"Wouldn't put it past her," he blurts. "She was seeing that punk ass kid while she was still with me."

"You mean her neighbor Mitch?"

His face grows colder—if that's even possible. "How do you know about that? Who are you? What's this about?"

"Know about that?" I ask. "So there's something to know?"

Jerrick regains his composure. "He crossed a line and I took care of it. That's it. Now do you want to tell me what you want?"

"So I take it you haven't heard about Abby?"

"Abby? What's wrong with her?" He steps forward and grabs the front of my shirt. "How do you know her?"

"I, um—she's a—" My brain seems to be wiped from his growing resistance. I should've expected this sort of reaction, but I didn't. I'm not good at this.

Chapter Six

"Jerrick!" someone calls from the office. "You've got a phone call."

"Who is it?" He lets go of me, but keeps his eyes locked with mine.

"The police," the man says quieter.

"I'll be right there," he hollers back, still watching me. When the office door closes again, he adds, "I think you know your way out."

———

SPRAWLED OUT ON the floor, I reach forward and grab the toe of my sneaker, feeling the muscles at the back of my leg stretch. After thirty seconds, I switch and do the same with the other leg.

Everyone else in the room is warming up. Stretching, chatting, getting ready for the next half hour of defense lessons. By and large, most of the people here are women, but luckily there is another man taking the class so I'm not the only one with a Y chromosome.

I started the self-defense classes shortly after Vernon died. I wanted to be sure I knew how to fight hand-to-hand in case I am ever without my powers or can't use them for whatever reason. If nothing else, it gives me another reason to get out of the house twice a week.

I already know the classes are helping because I've already tried a few moves on various criminals over the last few weeks. Plus, I have more confidence in the field, which is always helpful. There's no time to hesitate when you need to make a quick decision.

"All right, class, we're going to get started soon," the instructor says from the center of the mat. Tyrone is a buff black man in a black tank top and matching track pants. He was definitely intimidating to me during the first class, but I've come to realize that he's a nice guy.

We're in an old warehouse district near EIT. Most of the buildings in this area have been converted into something else: apartments, restaurants, coffee shops, trendy clothing stores. The redevelopment and its proximity to the campus has made this one of the hip neighborhoods in the city. This building in particular is now a multi-purpose gym filled with rooms for various forms of exercise and even a pool in the basement. These classes take place on the fourth floor and with the large floor-to-ceiling industrial windows, it offers fantastic views of Percival River running right through the evening's city lights.

"Gather around the mat, everyone." Tyrone stands at the edge and waits for everyone to form into a loose semi-circle. "Today we're going to work on attack postures. It's important to make sure your feet are planted firmly on the ground in order to maintain your balance and deliver the best attack. Now, I want you all to break into pairs and we'll get started."

The girl to my right immediately turns to me. She's new, I haven't seen her before. Her brown hair is pulled back into a ponytail and she's wearing yoga pants and a white tank top. She's short, too. Can't be much more than five feet tall. Her smile draws one from me too.

"Partners?" she asks.

I try to stop smiling, but it's no use. "Sure. I'm Ash."

She beams. "Melissa."

"All right," Tyrone says loudly as he meanders through the pairs. "I want one partner to stand there while the other partner charges them and tries to knock them down. No fists or kicks or anything. This is just a demonstration for now. Make sure you're away from the walls and that you have room to land on the mat."

I look over at Melissa. "I'll be the rock, you be the river."

"What?"

"Run at me." I stand with my feet shoulder-width apart and wait for the inevitable.

Chapter Six

She doesn't hold back as she charges, tucking her head down and jamming her shoulder into my belly. The impact makes me lose my balance and I collapse on the mat, breathless.

"Nice!" Tyrone calls to her from across the room. "That was an excellent tackle. Ash, next time I want you to push back once she hits you and make sure you stand your ground. Work on your defense reflexes as well."

I can feel everyone's eyes on me. Ignoring them, I get to my feet.

We try again. Like last time, she tucks her head down and charges at me. Because she's short, I don't have much to push back against so I fall to the mat once more.

"Again," Tyrone says, beside us now. "Keep practicing until you're both able to stand your ground."

Over and over again we go. Each time I fall hard on the mat. Finally, after the fifth time, I anticipate her move and hunker down as she charges, grabbing her by the shoulders and keeping her at bay. Both of our feet slide on the mat, but the force we exert on each other is the same.

"There you go!" Tyrone cheers.

He has us practice ways to disengage an attacker the rest of the class. Melissa is very skilled at all of them. Whether I have her in a headlock, have her wrists held behind her back, or have her pinned to the floor, she manages to work her way out of every situation.

"This isn't my first class," she admits halfway through with a smirk.

When it's my turn to go, it takes me a few more tries than Melissa, but I manage to break free from her hold too. And what strong holds she has. Despite her size, she has a lot of strength.

After class, I grab my water bottle from my bag and take a big gulp. These classes don't always make me sweaty, but they certainly leave me tired. Especially for the number of times that I've been knocked on my ass today.

"That was fun," Melissa says to my right. Her duffel bag is slung over her shoulder.

I chuckle. "Maybe for you."

"And yet you're still smiling."

I turn away in an effort to hide it, but I know it's no use. Together, we head down the stairs to the lobby on the ground floor.

"So what made you decide to take self-defense classes?" I ask.

She hooks an eyebrow. "I'm a short girl living by herself in the city. Having basic self-defense skills is important. I've been taking them for years."

That explains why she's so good at it.

"What about you?" she asks.

We reach the platform on the third floor and hook around to the next set of stairs.

"I got tired of being knocked down all the time."

She laughs. "Well, that hasn't changed yet."

"Guess not."

"So do you live around here?" she asks as we head down the last set of stairs.

I shake my head. "No, I live closer to downtown with a friend."

"Then what are you doing out here?"

I shrug. "It's the closest place I could find with quality self-defense classes."

"True." At the door to the street, she hesitates. "Well, you seem really nice. I'd love to hang out sometime."

My eyebrows shoot up. "Me?"

She chuckles again. "Yeah. You're cute."

Not what I was expecting, but I can't say that I'd *hate* the idea of hanging out with Melissa again. Especially in an environment where it won't be common practice for her to knock me down.

"Uh, okay," I stammer. "Yeah, that'd be fun."

She pulls out her phone. "What's your number? I'll text you

when I'm free."

I recite it and tell her I'll wait for her text. As I head back to the bus station I can't help but wonder if that was her way of asking me out on a date. She said 'hang out,' but does that mean something different? And shouldn't I have been the one to ask her if that's the case?

The possibility of a date makes me nervous. I try to cast it out of my mind, but it still persists. The giddy feeling wells up despite my efforts: she likes me!

———

WHEN I GET out of the shower later that night, Rachel's sitting on Perry's couch trying to pick a movie with him, who is on the floor. There's a bowl of popcorn between them.

"No, not anything gory," she says. "I see enough blood all day long, thank you very much."

"Then you should be used to it!" he counters. "If you don't want gory, what about funny?"

"Funny's good."

"The Hangover?"

She shoots him a look. "Not *stupid* funny. I like witty funny."

He rolls his eyes. "This is why we never invite you to movie night."

"Yeah, like Ash ever has any objections."

I move to the spot next to her, wiping away pieces of popcorn before I sit. "I'm a sponge that likes to take in all forms of our culture."

"See!" Perry shouts. "He thinks The Hangover is culture!"

"It's dumb. Pick something else." She looks over at me and says, "How'd the rest of your day go? Better than this morning?"

I shrug. "Abby's ex wouldn't really tell me anything. He did confirm that they broke up during their senior year of high school because she wanted to go to college, but I suspect there was more. Especially with her neighbor."

"What about her neighbor?"

"Her ex thought she was cheating on him."

"Was she?"

I shrug. "I don't know. Apparently Abby claimed she wasn't, but Sarah said she was hanging out with the boy who lived next door, who conveniently is also a student at EIT."

"Doesn't mean they're dating," Perry says.

"I know," I say. "Anyway, that's all I really know right now."

"Do you think her ex did it?" Rachel asks. "Because of the neighbor?"

I shrug. "I don't know. That's kind of what I think, but knowing that the police haven't moved in on him makes me doubt myself."

"Maybe they just don't have enough proof yet to arrest him," she offers. "Do you have anymore leads?"

"Just the guy she was supposedly cheating on the boyfriend with," I say. "I'm going to try to track him down tomorrow. I've called him a few times—even texted him—but I haven't gotten a response. Perry's going to check EIT's database tomorrow to see who these students are and what other connections they might have."

"Well, I'll see what I can do," Perry clarifies.

"What about you?" she asks.

"What *about* me?" I stare at her, challenging her to push me further about digging into my past. Luckily, Perry's quick to change the subject.

"Anyway, besides what happened this morning, my job is great," he says. "Thanks for asking, by the way. I know you were just dying to know. All the equipment in my lab is top of the line and I don't have to worry about the funding dropping out from under me. I'm on a three-year contract."

Rachel crosses her arms and stares at the TV. "Yeah, rub it in."

"Oh." The sarcasm fades from his voice. "I'm sorry. I didn't mean to—I'm sure there's probably room for growth at the hospital. At least within the Ellsworth Medical Group system."

"Yeah, I guess so, but that doesn't help me in the meantime," she says. "I just—I don't want to talk about it right now."

"Okay," he says. "Sorry I brought it up."

I clear my throat. "Well, on a different note, I got a job offer today."

"You did?" Rachel asks.

"Yeah, you never told me exactly what it was for," Perry adds. I left that detail out earlier because Abby's death was the bigger part of that story.

"It's only part time," I say. "Hopefully under the table."

"Well yeah, you don't know where your other identification documents are," he cuts in.

"Not until he digs into his past," she adds.

"I get it, I get it. I'll find all that out eventually. For now, though, I have this offer that I'm not sure if I'm even going to take."

"Why not?" Rachel asks.

"Because of the murders. How am I supposed to find out who did this to them if I'm stuck at work?"

She rolls her eyes. "Ash, that's not your responsibility."

"I'm Heat, so it kind of is."

"He's got a point," Perry says. "But, I agree with Rachel. I think you should take the job. I'm assuming it's with Lisa?"

"Lisa from Vernon's party?" Rachel asks.

"Yeah, she works in the lab next to Perry now as a secretary for one of the researchers."

"Hmm, that's interesting. When did she start that?"

"I guess shortly after Vernon's party," I say. "Anyway, it'd be almost like a lab assistant for Dr. Henry Isaacs. Cleaning, setting up, checking inventory. It's not that big of a deal."

"It's something," he says.

"Oh, Dr. Isaacs?"

"Do you know him?" I ask.

"I've read a couple of his articles," she says. "He's got some interesting theories."

My brow furrows. "Interesting good or interesting bad?"

She shrugs. "I don't really remember the details. But I agree with Perry. I think this will be good to get you out and about. And Lisa's a really nice person."

"We'd be work neighbors!" Perry beams.

I crack a smile. "Yeah, we would."

"It sounds like a sweet deal," he says.

"Besides your self-defense classes, what other reason do you have to leave this apartment?" she asks.

"Heat stuff," I say.

"You need a life outside of Heat," Rachel says. "Have you made any friends at your class?"

I start to shake my head, but stop myself. "Well, sort of. Today I was partnered with this new girl and she asked me to hang out sometime."

"Oooo!" Perry teases. "Ash has a date!"

"It's not a date!"

Rachel smirks. "Did she give you her number?"

"No, I gave her mine. She said she was going to text me."

She studies her fingernails. "Sounds like a date to me."

"It's not a date!" I repeat, louder this time.

Perry glances at Rachel. "Looks like we'll be back to a duo once Ash starts getting some."

She makes a face. "Must you?"

He puts up his hands. "Hey, I'm just saying."

"Okay!" I shout. "Let's just pick a movie!"

CHAPTER SEVEN

"Just be confident," Perry tells me the next morning when we get to his lab. "You've got this."

I let out a deep breath and try to keep my hands from shaking. I've been trying to build up the nerve to talk to Lisa about the job she offered me yesterday. With everything that's happened in the last twenty-four hours, it feels like yesterday morning was so long ago. But life goes on and so should I.

After talking to Rachel and Perry last night, I figured it was probably the best move to pacify them—mainly Rachel. She was and will be the most persistent about trying to figure out who I am. Plus, this job would give me a reason to be on campus in case anything else pops up that might lead to identifying the murderer.

"She offered you the job, so it's not like she's going to say no." Perry takes a seat at his desk and boots up his computer.

I stand in front of his desk and fidget with the pens in the cup holder at the corner. "Actually, she said she needed to talk to Dr. Isaacs before I got the official okay. So it's not a sure thing. Maybe he said no."

He gives me a look. "I'm sure it's fine. Would you stop that?"

I pull my hand away from the pens and cross my arms. "Sorry. Just nervous."

"Don't be. It'll be fine. Jeez, you're acting like this is some top-level executive job. It's just a lab cleaner."

"It's the only job I've ever had—or can remember having."

In an effort to stall further, I look around the room. His lab isn't as big as the one he and Rachel shared at ESTR, which is ironic because there are four people working out of here, including Perry. His desk sits side-by-side with another researcher's desk. On the opposite end of the room, two other desks face each other.

Next to Perry's desk is a wall full of cabinets and in the middle of the room is an island counter with a sink. A large fluorescent light hangs over it next to an electrical outlet hanging from the ceiling. When Perry first interviewed here, he said the building hadn't been renovated in nearly fifty years and was in need of an update. I can certainly see why.

The limited space to move in here is probably a fire violation just waiting to be issued. Clearly, they didn't intend for this many researchers to be working out of one lab. I'm surprised the police didn't mention anything after they cleared out of here. Then again, they had more important things on their minds.

"Did everyone enjoy their day off yesterday?" Barry walks in with a coffee in one hand and a banana in the other. He takes his seat across the room from Perry.

"Yeah, if you count wasting half the day in the lounge," Perry mutters.

I look around for signs of the body. The tile floors have been sufficiently scrubbed and the sand has all been swept away. "They cleaned everything up, at least."

Chapter Seven

"There wasn't much to clean up," Barry says. "The sand was the worst part."

"Yeah, what was with that?" Perry asks him. "Did you hear anymore about what happened? Who it was?"

Barry shakes his head. "Not a word. All I know is what I told you yesterday."

If he does know more, he's probably hesitant to tell Perry with me standing right here. As an outsider who's only met him a few times, I haven't gained the trust of workplace gossip. Perry's barely gained that trust, but it's a good thing that he has. It's my cue to leave. Whatever Perry finds out, he'll relay to me.

Hooking my thumb over my shoulder, I say, "I'm going to go talk to Lisa. I'll see you guys later."

I step out into the hall and turn to Dr. Isaacs' door to the right. After knocking twice, I slowly open it and step inside.

"Ash, hi!" Lisa jumps up from her seat when she sees me. She offers a bright smile and waves me inside. "Come on in!"

Although Perry's lab is probably a little bigger, Dr. Isaacs' is more spacious since he's the only researcher occupying it. With the exception of Lisa's desk in the corner, the whole space is mostly free of obstructions and more in line with what Lab #8 at ESTR used to look like.

"How are you?" I return her smile. "Have you heard anymore from Sarah?"

She shakes her head. "Not since I walked her back to her building yesterday. I didn't want to take her all the way to her room because we're not supposed to be in the dorms, but I kind of wish I would have. I just can't imagine what she's going through."

I nod. "Yeah, I know. I'm sure her parents came as soon as they heard."

"I hope so. She said she was going to call them right away. I was thinking of maybe trying to get in touch with her to check up on her, but she's probably getting bombarded with all kinds of phone calls and stuff."

Like the way I hunted her down yesterday. I'm not really proud of that, but I got what I wanted, I guess.

"It's probably better to give her some time to process it all." As if I'm one to talk.

"Yeah," she agrees.

I take a look around. "So this is it, huh?"

She follows my gaze. "It's a bit of a change from my cubicle downtown, but I like to think of it as cozier."

"You mean, despite how sterile it is?" I motion up to the tiny window near the ceiling. "And that's not to mention all the natural light in here."

She laughs. "That stale smell kind of grows on you. So does the window."

"I guess it'd have to."

"Anyway, I'm glad you're here," she says. "Since the lab was still off-limits when Dr. Isaacs finished with classes yesterday, I got to talk to him about what you and I discussed yesterday."

My stomach flutters. "Yeah? What did he say?"

"Well, he liked the idea right away, but he was concerned about where we'd find the money because I told him you'd prefer it to be under the table."

I swallow hard. Maybe it wasn't a good idea to tell her that. But there's no other way I can be paid.

"He told me to figure out where we could pull the funds from and he'd think about it. So last night I took the ledger home and did some finessing with the finances until I freed some up for you."

"Oh, I don't want to take away money from anything that's important."

She waves it off. "It's fine. Everything worked out, so now the offer is official. What about you? Have you given it anymore thought?"

"Um…uh, yeah, I have." I'm flustered, trying not to appear

too excited. "I think it would be a great fit."

"Perfect! I think I told you yesterday, but it would be ideal if you could work in the mornings while Dr. Isaacs is teaching so that everything's set up for him when he comes down in the afternoons to work. Is that okay?"

"That's fine with me. How soon do you need me to start?"

"Tomorrow? I mean, it's all pretty simple so there really isn't much in the way of training. Or we could say next week if you want to wait. If you're really jonesing to get going, you could even start right now."

"Oh okay." That was much sooner than I expected, but with limited leads for the murders, I don't have much else to do this morning. "Yeah, I can start now."

"Are you sure?" she asks. "There's no rush. The ball's kind of in your court now."

"No, I'm free so it's really no problem."

"Okay!" She smiles. "Let me give you a quick tour. Dr. Isaacs is the Substances and Particles Specialist, so he works with all kinds of solutions and mixtures, which requires proper cleanup. Be prepared for rubber gloves and maybe even a smock when you're down here. You'll thank me later."

"Got it."

"None of it should be harmful or anything, but it's still safer to go through the precautions of disposing any spills or leaks in a biohazard trash, just in case. For the most part, though, you'll just be washing beakers, scrubbing countertops, and setting up supplies for whatever he needs that day."

"Sounds easy enough."

"It's not going to be the most exciting job, but hopefully you'll see that you're a vital part of the process." She moves around the island counter in the center of the room. It has a sink in it just like in Perry's lab. She motions to the cabinets on the back wall. "This is where we keep all of the supplies." She opens a door and I glance inside. "It's messy, so if you have extra time,

I don't think anybody would be mad if you came up with some sort of organizational system. But I'd wait until you get a feel for what Dr. Isaacs uses most and how he thinks."

"Okay then. Wait on rearranging stuff. What's next?"

She moves down to the far wall, which has open shelving filled with buckets and boxes. In the corner is another desk with a computer. Likely Dr. Isaacs'. Beside that in the corner, is a stack of boxes, buckets, and containers marked "FRAGILE" or "TOX-IC" or "DO NOT CONSUME."

"This is where we keep all the shipments that come in," Lisa explains. "He tells me what he needs for different experiments, I source it and order it and we stick it over here until he's ready to use it. Some of this he uses frequently." Her hands hover over some of the labels on the boxes. "Uh…saline, sodium chloride, calcium oxide, whatever. Those he uses all the time, so just keep an eye on the inventory levels of those. I usually check, but it doesn't hurt to have a second set of eyes. And if you can find a better place to put this all instead of stacked in the corner, that would be ideal."

"I'll try to come up with something."

She points to the opposite corner next to Dr. Isaacs' desk. "The cabinet over there has all of our cleaning supplies. Generally, we let the custodial staff clean up in here, but for spills and leaks, we have everything on hand. Again, if you need something, let me know and I'll contact the custodians for replacements. Sounds easy enough?"

I nod. "Yes, ma'am."

"Oh, just call me Lisa. No need for formalities here. Do you have any questions?"

Looking around, I replay everything she's told me in my head. "No, I think that's it."

"If you think of something, just ask."

"Okay. What do you want me to start with?"

"Why don't you wash out the beakers in the sink? There's

a pair of rubber gloves in the cabinet, just to be safe. I'll come up with a list of things you can do after you're done with that, okay?"

"Sounds good."

I spend the rest of the day being a glorified maid. After the beakers are cleaned, I move to the cleaning closet and start organizing that for my own sanity. Dr. Isaacs might not notice it, but it'll help me do a better job while I'm here. Plus, it's good practice for when I have to organize all of his solutions and stuff.

At noon I finish up, offering a wave to Perry through the open door as I pass by his lab. I get one foot on the bottom step of the staircase that leads out of the basement, but down the hall in the opposite direction I catch sight of a utility closet open with a custodial cart parked outside. From the commotion I hear in the closet, I know there's someone in there. Another janitor. Maybe someone who knew the student who was killed in Perry's lab.

"Excuse me?" I knock lightly on the door that's open as I peer inside.

An older man in a gray jumpsuit turns when he hears me. He has silver hair and a bushy mustache. The name tag on his chest tells me his name is Charlie. He offers a friendly smile.

"Yes, sir. Do you need something?" he asks.

"Well, sort of," I start. "I don't want to be nosy or anything, but I was just wondering if you knew the student who was attacked down here?"

Best not to use words like "killed," "body," or "victim." I don't know who had a deeper connection with him and mentioning his attack might stir up feelings that would get in the way of getting me answers. As cold and callous as that sounds.

His expression turns grim. "Yes, I did. He was a good kid. Didn't know him long—maybe a week—but he was a good worker."

"Do you mind telling me his name?"

Charlie pulls away a little and looks like he's about to object, but I add quickly, "I would like to write his family a sympathy card. Other than rumors and the police cars outside yesterday, I haven't really heard anything."

He nods slowly. "The school is keeping this hush-hush, which is a shame. The kid probably had a lot of friends. Not to mention his family." He rubs his stubbly chin, considering. Finally, he says, "I'll tell you what; I'll give you his name if you promise to keep it to yourself. I understand you want to reach out, but if the school wants to keep it quiet, I don't want to get anyone mad. I'm only a year out from retirement."

I nod. "Sure, of course."

"He was Mitch Mantel. A freshman, I believe. Just started working for us last week."

Mitch Mantel, as in the one I've been trying to call because of his connection with Abby. Interesting.

"Any idea who might've done it?" I ask.

Charlie shakes his head. "No. Like I said, I didn't really know him. He was pretty quiet, but always nice. Polite. I can't imagine why anyone would want to hurt him."

"That's horrible." I try to feign ignorance.

"Actually, wait. There was something a few days ago."

I raise my eyebrows. "What?"

"It was probably nothing," he says. "I just saw him and one of the researchers down here arguing about something."

"Who was he arguing with?"

"I don't know his name. He was younger than me—not that that's saying much." He chuckles. "But he was bald and had a red beard."

Sounds like Perry's friend Barry Murphy. Odd. He told Perry that he didn't know much.

"Do you know what they were arguing about?"

Charlie shakes his head. "No, sorry. I wish I did, with what happened and all. Anything that I could do to help, but sometimes you're just helpless, you know?"

I nod sympathetically. "Now, I've heard rumors that there was sand all over. It seems made up, but it's curious, isn't it?"

"Curious? It's downright weird," he says. "I saw it myself!"

"Did you see him? Before the police came, that is."

He shakes his head. "No, someone else must've. I was working Jasper yesterday, but I was called over to clean up the sand after the police moved out."

"Oh, and that's how you saw the sand."

Charlie nods. "And it was *everywhere*."

"So do you have any idea how Mitch was…you know…"

"Killed? Not a clue. There wasn't any blood from what I could see. No idea what the hell happened, but it didn't appear to be…messy, in that respect. No bruising or anything, from what I've heard. And his cart, broom, bucket, all of his stuff was still right there with him. He was just doing his job. Besides the sand, it looked like he might've just had a heart attack or something. But at *eighteen*?" He shakes his head. "I can't imagine that's what happened."

"Strange."

He scoffs. "You said it, kid."

"Well, thank you for the talk," I say. "I'll make sure to get the card out real soon."

"Of course, yeah," he says. "I appreciate you thinking of those affected by this. It's…it's a tragedy."

Chapter Eight

W ho are you?" Pat Zarek asks when he answers the door to his dorm. Behind him is a small narrow room with a window at the end and matching sets of furniture on either side: two beds, two desks, two dressers.

"My name is Ash," I tell him. "I was hoping I could talk to you about your roommate. Do you mind if I come in?"

"Are you with the police?"

I glance down the hall to see if anyone's giving me a weird look. If I'm caught in the dorms I'll likely be arrested. I was able to sneak in by following a student inside. Luckily, I somehow look like I'm still a college student so me being here isn't that unusual of a sight.

"No, I'm just someone who wants to help," I tell him. "Please. I think you might be able to help me connect some dots the police are missing."

He nods and stands back to allow me to enter.

When I step into the room, the smell of independent teenage

hygiene hits me. Tucked beside the dresser is an overflowing bag of laundry and I nearly trip on the old pizza box leaning against the wall near the door.

Pat follows my gaze. "Sorry." He snatches up the bag and stuffs it under his bed, as if that takes care of the smell. "Yesterday was supposed to be laundry day but with what happened…"

I nod. "I get it. Mind if I sit down?"

He pulls out the chair from Mitch's desk as an offering and I take a seat as he plops in his own. Looking at Mitch's desk, I see the standard essentials: an old mug in the corner stuffed with shiny-new pens, markers, and pencils. Along the back of the desk are other office supplies: a stapler, three-hole-puncher, and a picture of a black lab panting under a giant oak tree with the sun streaming through the branches.

"No computer?" I ask.

"Uh, no," he says. "The police took it as evidence."

Right. Obviously they were already here.

"Any idea why?"

"No. He was working on it every day, though. Even before classes started."

"What was he working on?"

"I don't really know. He was just typing in a Word document, rereading it, rewriting it. I never asked what it was."

"Scholarships? Pre-course homework?"

"I don't know."

"Do you know if he ever printed it off or if he has another copy somewhere else that I might be able to read?"

"No, he never printed it," Pat responds. "As far as I know, whatever it was that he was working on is on the computer that the police took."

"Okay. Did they take anything else?"

He shrugs. "I don't know. I wasn't really paying attention. One of them was talking to me while the other was going through his stuff. People were passing by in the hall making comments.

Some of them have been knocking on my door, trying to get the gossip."

"So why'd you let me in?"

"I was getting tired of all the conspiracy theories I was hearing. That Mitch ODed, that he was suicidal. None of it is true. I didn't know him long, but Mitch and I were becoming friends. It's horrible what happened to him. I don't know *exactly* what happened, but I know that's not it."

"How can you be sure?"

"He seemed happy."

"Sometimes people who've made the decision to take their life seem happy because they think they've found a solution."

Pat's already shaking his head before I finish. "No, not Mitch. He made friends easily. Everyone liked him. He seemed to have a good relationship with his dad, they talked every night. And that girl who died, they were friends too."

Just like Sarah said.

"Did you ever meet Abby?" I ask.

"Once, when she stopped by to talk to Mitch," he responds. "It was the day after we moved in. I thought it was weird that he already had girls coming to see him, but he said they went to high school together."

"Were they dating?"

He shakes his head again. "I don't think so. Actually, I think Mitch might've been gay."

"Why do you say that?"

"The way he talked, the people he hung out with—I don't know." He runs his finger along the metal frame of the chair. "It was just the feeling I got. I could be wrong, though."

"Either way, you don't think he and Abby were together?"

"No, they always seemed serious when they met up. Never really joked or showed any kind of affection. I thought they had had a fight. The longer I got to know Mitch, the more I started to think he was…you know."

Chapter Eight

"What did they talk about?"

"I don't know. They always left the room or went somewhere where no one could hear them when they talked."

"Did they hang out any other time?"

"Not really," he says. "He said they were neighbors, but they didn't seem like friends. At least not here."

So now two people say Abby and Mitch weren't dating. But a lot of time passed between when Abby and Jim broke up in the middle of their senior year until the first week of college. Maybe Abby and Mitch dated, broke up, and were only trying to negotiate returning each other's things.

My gut is telling me it's more than that, though. Especially if Pat is saying that he suspects Mitch didn't even like girls.

"You said everyone liked Mitch?"

He nods. "Uh huh. He was friends with a lot of people."

"Was there anyone he wasn't friends with? Maybe even hated?"

"Not that I know of. I mean, he said he got in a fight with one guy in high school, but that was all he said."

"When did he tell you that?"

"His dad came to pick him up for a doctor appointment," he explains. "I guess whatever happened to him during that fight required a few checkups."

"So he was hurt pretty bad then?"

From what I can remember, Jim Jerrick is a decent-sized guy who could probably throw a punch. Or maybe swing some mechanic tools as a weapon. Of course, that doesn't explain how Mitch ended up dead without a scratch but surrounded by sand. Not unless Jerrick developed powers somehow, which is possible. Anything's possible.

"I guess so," Pat says.

"Any idea who that guy was?"

He shakes his head again. "He didn't say."

I drop my hands to my knees and rise to my feet. "Okay,

well, you've been a big help. I'll be in touch if I have anymore questions."

"Ash?" Pat says when I turn to the door.

"Yeah?"

"I hope someone figures out who did this," he says. "Mitch was a good person. He didn't deserve to die so young."

I offer a sad smile. "No, he didn't. I'll do the best I can."

———

THE STEAM RISES from my cup of coffee as I sit at the counter along the front window of the coffee shop on North River Avenue. Since it's directly across from Paul's Auto, it gives me the perfect hideout to wait for Jim Jerrick to get out of work.

Based off of what Pat told me, I know that Jerrick and Mitch not only had history, but have spilled some blood over Abby. Maybe knowing that they're still in contact set Jerrick off on a rage. Which gave him a reason to kill Mitch.

Now all I need to do is see if he has powers. Cornering him as Heat should do the trick. I have my suit on under my clothes and the mask stuffed in my bag. I'm ready to go whenever he is.

Across the street, Jerrick and another man move around the shop. Packing up tools, moving cars around, sweeping the floor. Looks like they're about to close up for the day.

Thank God.

I take a sip of my third cup of coffee. I've been here for at least three hours, only leaving my post to order more coffee and take care of my bladder, which demanded immediate attention. I couldn't risk Jerrick sneaking off early, but I guess my overkill was unnecessary. My hand quivers; whether from the caffeine or nerves, it's hard to say.

At five o'clock on the dot, the garage doors on the front of the shop come down. My cue to move. I head straight out the door and around to the back of the coffee house, stripping my clothes off until I'm down to my Heat suit. After I pull on my mask, I stash my bag behind the dumpster and race around to the front again.

Swinging his keys casually in his hand, Jerrick goes to a beat-up sedan parked on the street. Squinting at the bright afternoon sun, he waits for a car to pass before getting behind the wheel. It's the same car I saw parked on the street yesterday when I visited him. He pulls away from the curb and I burst into flame and lift in the air, keeping my eye on his car as it navigates the tight city streets.

There isn't a cloud in sight, so there's no place for me to hide. Luckily, most people are hypnotized by their desire to get home and don't pay any attention to the flaming man flying through the air. Not that I'd know if someone spotted me from inside their car.

Eventually, Jerrick travels out of the tight city streets into suburbia. It takes him less than ten minutes to get to an apartment complex just off the expressway. He pulls into a parking spot at one of the buildings in the back of the complex. Zooming straight down to the pavement, I land hard and run at him the moment the flames disperse.

Out of the corner of his eye, he spots me and breaks into a run toward the door marked 196. His keys jangle as he struggles to find the right one to enter his apartment.

Easing up now that he doesn't have anywhere to hide, I step toward him slowly, letting his anxiety build. If he's fearful, he's more likely to answer anything I ask him. At least, that's my hope.

Finally, his door swings open and he dashes inside. Breaking into a sprint, I try to catch it before he closes it in my face.

Too late.

Taking a few steps back, I charge at the door in an attempt to break it, but it holds firm. Once, twice, three times I try, but it's no use. The longer the bastard is out of my sight, the more time he has to find a weapon or an accomplice. Or set up a trap to kill me the same way he did Mitch and Abby.

Letting my anger flow through me, I raise my foot and drive it straight into the door near the handle. The doorjamb finally gives way and the door swings open, slamming against the wall.

I step inside the quiet, still apartment and look around. It's a prefab, cookie-cutter style space and isn't filled with very much furniture. There's the secondhand couch and the cardboard box serving as the TV stand in the space just inside the door. Further back, there's a single bar stool at the kitchen counter, even though there appears to be room for at least two more.

Noise from the kitchen on the opposite end of the room puts me on full alert. A drawer opening and then closing. It's soft, but I hear it.

I step around the counter and see Jerrick cowering behind the cabinets. All the bravado from yesterday vanished. His shoulders are hunched and his hands shake. Droplets of sweat dribble down the sides of his face.

"You killed Mitch Mantel, didn't you?" I reach for the front of his shirt and lift him to his feet.

"What? What are you talking about?" He holds firm to the knife in his hand, which he doesn't raise to me or threaten me with.

I look into his eyes, seeing more details than I saw yesterday when I first talked to him. There are dark circles under his eyes, scabs all over his arms. Now that I see him in the sunlight streaming through the window, his skin looks sallow. Almost as if he's older than he is. Actually, if it wasn't for Jerrick acknowledging that he dated Abby, I'd be wondering if I even had the right guy.

Staring into his eyes, watching as he cowers for *his* life as if the lives of Mitch and Abby didn't matter ignites rage deep inside me.

I throw him across the counter and he collides with the lone bar stool on the other side before crashing to the floor. "You killed Mitch Mantel because he was seeing Abby Adams!" I bark at him. "Admit it."

"No!" he shouts. "It wasn't me! I swear! I haven't seen her in months! Or him!"

With another fistful of his shirt, I yank him back to his feet, driving him into the wall and creating a dent in the drywall. "And then you killed Abby because you couldn't stand the thought of her being with anyone else but you, huh?"

"No!" His hands fumble worse now and the knife he was clutching drops to the carpeted floor.

"Suffocated her with sand, just like you did to Mitch," I continue, ignoring him. "Why don't you come at me the same way you did him, huh?"

"I don't know what you're talking about, man," he whimpers. "I didn't kill nobody!"

Spinning him around, I grab his arm and yank it up his back. I push him down over the counter and shout in his ear, "Liar!"

"AHH! I'm not lying! I wasn't even—it couldn't have been me!"

"Why not?" I murmur between clenched teeth.

Pulling his arm up higher results in more screams from Jerrick. I'm dangerously close to breaking it. This has to be intense pain. If this doesn't make him crack, I'll have to try another tactic.

"Tell me!" I bark again.

"I've been—it wasn't me!"

Pushing his arm a millimeter higher sends another scream out of him.

"I've been high every night this week," he shouts. "The needles are in the kitchen sink!"

I release him and stand back so he can stand up straight. He spins around and cradles his arm. There's terror in his eyes.

Keeping a close watch on him, I step back to the kitchen and inspect the sink. Just as he said, there are several syringes sitting at the bottom of the stainless steel.

"They died at that school, right?" He massages his arm. "I seen it on the news yesterday."

"What's your point?" I hold out my hand and create a small ball of fire that flickers like a lit candle.

He lets out a high-pitched squeal when he sees it. "I haven't ever stepped foot at that place! I swear to you!"

I take another step forward and he cowers further.

"Yeah, I did have some words with that Mitch guy last year— even traded a few punches—"

"You did more than just trade a few punches."

He lets out a deep breath. "Okay, I hurt him pretty bad. But that was it. I didn't kill him."

"What made you stop? I mean, Abby was still talking to him, still broken up with you. Must've been a pretty big hit to your massive ego."

His eyes glance down to the fireball in my hand and then back up to me. "His dad threatened to press charges, so I backed off."

I nod to the sink. "Found a new hobby, did you?"

"Beats going to jail for assault."

As I raise the ball of fire as a threat, Jerrick cowers backward and lets out another involuntary whimper that causes me to stop dead in my tracks.

Suddenly, I'm seeing myself through his eyes: I'm a monster who just followed him home and broke into his house to terrorize him. He's told me what he knows and where he was. He can't tell me what's not true. What more do I expect to get out of him? How much more pain would I put him through in my desperate attempt to find Mitch and Abby's killer?

That's not what a hero is and it's not who I am. This has gotten out of hand. I need to get out of here. The murderer had abilities like I do. If Jerrick was that person, he would've played that card by now. He isn't who I'm looking for.

Chapter Eight

Stepping back, I stifle the flame. I swallow hard, trying to push away my pride. "Make sure I don't ever have another reason to come after you." I glance over at the sink. "And find a new hobby."

Without waiting for an answer, I run out the door and fly away from Jerrick's apartment.

Chapter Nine

At Rachel's doorstep I knock hard three times. After what just happened with Jerrick, it's the only place where I know I won't feel worse about myself. Despite how Rachel might feel about me trying to find the murderer, she'll listen to where my head's at.

The door swings open and she smiles.

"Come on in." She stands aside to allow me to pass by and closes the door behind me. "It's a good thing you texted me first." She walks behind the counter into the kitchen and pulls a whistling tea kettle off the stove.

"Why's that?" I take a seat at one of the stools near the counter.

She lets out a big breath. "Oh, Evan and I have been arguing lately."

"I'm sorry."

She shrugs it off. "It's all right. It's just—no offense, but seeing you would not have been good for his mood."

"Oh, right. Is it about anything big?" As soon as the words leave my mouth, I wish they hadn't. "Sorry, I don't mean to pry."

Rachel doesn't seem to mind. "No, you're fine. It's probably a good idea I talk things out with someone anyway." She fills two mugs with hot water and carries one over to me. "It's dumb, really. We're fighting about money. Or rather, the lack thereof." She sets a small basket of tea bags in front of me. "Help yourself."

I select a green tea, rip off the packaging, and dunk the bag into my cup. "Is he mad that you lost your job?"

"Well, sort of." She dips her tea bag in the steaming water, watching as it darkens with flavor. "He knows it's not my fault. I mean, the place literally burned down. It's just it's pretty obvious that he wishes things we're different."

"Did he say anything?"

"Not in so many words, but it was implied."

"I'm sorry. If it wasn't for me, you and Perry would both still be working there."

"Ash, it's not your fault. You didn't start the fire."

"I know, but it still kind of is my fault," I counter. "I should've lured the Gatekeeper out of the building. I should've been able to put out the fire—"

"As far as we know, your ability only allows you to create fire, not stifle it."

"Yeah, but I still feel like I should've done something."

"Even if you did save the building, there's nothing saying our funding would still be there," she says. "Vernon was our rep with River Valley. Since he died—and since Arlus Cain knew *you* knew you two were brothers—I doubt the funding would've continued. At least for our lab. There would've been some baloney explanation."

"Yeah, maybe you're right. No sense debating the what-ifs." I take a careful sip of my tea. Still too hot. "I just can't help but feel like when I arrived, everything changed for you guys."

She offers a warm smile. "Despite what the initial setbacks

might portray, I know that things changed for the better with you. Think of all the people you've saved."

"Yeah." I stare at my cup.

"Even though I needed to take a pay cut, I feel a better sense of security with my new job because I *know* the funding will still be there next year, and the year after."

"Too bad your boyfriend doesn't see it that way."

She sighs. "He's just frustrated because he wants to go out and do things, but since I'm on a budget I can't afford to do anything. That's why lately every time you and I have hung out with Perry, it's been either here or at his place."

"And Evan can't foot the bill while you're going through this?"

Rachel shakes her head. "That's not fair to him and it's certainly not a habit I want to get into. I don't want to get comfortable with this job. To an extent, I want to feel the financial burden to motivate me to find a better one."

"I guess I can see that," I say. "But I don't think I'd make the same decision."

She chuckles and leans forward on the counter as she cradles her mug. "Fair enough. But I'm determined to be as independent as possible."

"Well, you have been." I motion around the room. "You have this house to show for it."

"Yeah," she murmurs.

"What? Are you wishing you hadn't bought it?"

"No, it's not that."

I wait for her to continue, but she doesn't. "So what is it?"

After another sip, she says, "I probably shouldn't be telling you this, but during our last fight Evan suggested that I sell the house and move someplace cheaper."

"What did you say?"

"I flat out told him no."

"Yeah, you worked hard for this house. You shouldn't have

to give it up unless you decide to."

"Exactly! The problem is, the jerk put the idea in my head and now I'm wondering if I'm just putting myself in more trouble by staying here. He has a point. There are plenty of cheaper options available. Maybe I'm just being foolish holding onto this. It's just a house."

"But it's not," I say. "It's a symbol of your independence, of everything you've accomplished. Not just that, but it's your *home*. Believe me, when you don't have a home, it's something you crave."

She gives me a sad smile. Kind words are all we can offer each other at this point, but words won't fix our problems.

"Anyway, that's probably not what you came here to talk about." She stands up straighter and leans her hip against the counter. "What's up?"

"Well first off, I want you to go into this conversation with an open mind."

She narrows her eyes, already skeptical.

"It's about the murders."

To my surprise, she doesn't say anything. Although the way she sets her mug down and crosses her arms as she studies me says enough.

"I thought I had it narrowed down to one very obvious killer, but it turns out I was wrong."

Her face turns to worry. "Ash, what did you do?"

I ignore her and go on. "The two victims knew each other."

"Were they dating?"

"Not according to either of their roommates."

"Friends?"

"Maybe, but Mitch's roommate said he never saw them really hanging out. And Abby's ex-boyfriend beat up Mitch last year because he *thought* they were together."

"So I take you looked into the ex?" she asks.

"Yeah. They broke up because she wanted to go to college."

"Well, judging from the way you started this story, I'm going to say that the ex was not the guy who did it."

I shake my head. "No, he wasn't."

She shrugs. "So look into Mitch's exes. Look into their roommates. Look at some of their classmates. See if the victims had anything they were hiding."

"I think they did."

"Why's that?"

"The police confiscated Mitch's computer. Probably Abby's too. And their cell phones."

"That might just be standard practice," she says. "See who they were talking to and what they were doing right before their deaths. It's a communication gold mine for them."

"Or it could mean that there's something on those computers."

"Like what?"

I shake my head. "I don't know yet. Mitch's roommate said he was always working on something on his laptop, even before classes started."

"Kids are always on their computers," she says. "It could be nothing."

"Or it could be something. I just don't know how to figure out what it is he was doing."

"The roommate didn't have any idea?"

"No."

"What about Abby's roommate?"

"She didn't mention anything like that."

"Doesn't mean Abby wasn't working on something similar," Rachel counters. "These two were killed for a reason. *Something* not only links them but also gave someone else reason to kill them. One way or another, the truth will come out. The question is, how many more people are going to die before that happens?"

As if I didn't already have that weighing on me. I run my hand through my hair and study the clean white countertop. I've been racking my brain over this ever since Abby was killed. And jumping to a conclusion almost resulted in me seriously hurting an innocent man.

"Not getting the right guy isn't what I'm worried about," I admit. "At least, not at this moment."

"Then what is it?"

"I—I scared myself today. I went too far."

Her voice softens. "What do you mean?"

"I followed Abby's ex home as Heat and things got out of hand."

Her eyes grow wide. "Ash, did you start his house on fire?"

I shake my head again. "No, nothing like that. I, uh…I almost broke his arm. I didn't believe him when he said he didn't do anything. I *wanted* it to be him. For it to be that simple. But it wasn't him and I just kept going after him as if that would change his answer. I could've really hurt him, Rach."

Reaching across the counter, she squeezes one of my hands. "So what stopped you?"

"I realized that he was only fighting back as a person."

"As opposed to…?"

"As opposed to the super who killed those students."

She pulls her hand away. "How do you know it was a super?"

"The sand. The fact that Sarah was only separated from Abby for a short while—maybe a few seconds—and Abby died in that timeframe. There was no blood on either of the victims, no bruising, no history of heart conditions or anything else that could cause what the police have ruled as death by asphyxiation."

"Where did you hear that?"

"One of Perry's co-workers overheard it. Rachel, this isn't a normal murder. I'm looking for someone who's like me: different."

She rests her chin on her fist and stares at the countertop without saying anything.

"Not to mention the fact that the ex said he was high when

Mitch and Abby died," I add. "I saw the needles. I saw the scars. He's an addict. It wasn't him."

She keeps her eyes down, still silent.

"Please say something, Rach."

Finally, she looks at me and leans across the counter to grab both of my hands. "All right, I'm going to put my psychiatrist hat on because I feel like that's the real reason you came here to begin with. Now don't get mad, just hear me out."

Wordlessly, I nod.

"I feel like you're so invested in these murders because it's a way to distract yourself from the realities of your own life," she says.

"You mean my non-existent life?"

"I mean the one that you're refusing to remember," she counters. "You're worried about what you'll uncover. Are you really a good person? Maybe you don't actually have any other family besides Arlus. Maybe your current situation will not instantly be fixed by reuniting with your family and friends. These are all valid fears, Ash. Nobody's blaming you for being hesitant."

Well, she just laid it all out there. I can't say I disagree with her, though. She has a point. I *have* been reluctant to search through my own history and Arlus *is* the biggest reason. So far, he's the only example I have of what my life is really like and I'm not a fan of that example. I want better. I feel like I deserve better.

"I have this theory—and there's nothing really supporting this theory other than my intuition—but I think your loss of memories is psychological, not biological," she says.

I furrow my brow. "What do you mean?"

"Well, based off the research I did back at ESTR, I found that physically you're perfectly healthy. Even with the elevated mercury levels that give you your powers."

"So you think there's some traumatic event in my past that I'm blocking out, and by default I'm blocking out everything else as well?"

Chapter Nine

She shrugs. "It's just a theory."

Yeah, but a damn good one.

"Look, I get it if you're not ready," she says. "I just want you to be cautious so you don't go overboard and get yourself in trouble with these student murders."

"I get that. And I appreciate it, but I do feel like I need to help figure out who killed these students because I can. I have these powers so I might as well use them to help people. If someone else with their own set of powers attacks anyone and I *didn't* help them, that would be guilt that would weigh on me for the rest of my life." I tap at my chest. "*I* can help, so that's what I'm going to do."

She smiles and squeezes my hand. "This is how I know you have nothing to worry about with your past. You're a good person, Ash. When you're ready to find out what else makes you *you*, I'll help you in whatever way I can."

I return her smile. "Thanks Rachel. And you're right. I guess I am afraid of what I'll find, but there's no way to know until I start looking. And I think I know the best place to start."

Chapter Ten

My shadow stretches out in front of me as I walk across campus from the parking lot to the Herbert Science Building. EIT is eerily quiet. I'm only a little earlier than normal, but apparently that makes a difference. When I get down to the basement of Herbert, I see the light in Dr. Isaacs' lab is already on. I thought I was going to have to hang out in the lounge until Lisa got here. Either that or track down a janitor who would open the door for me.

Peeking inside the room before I step in, I spot a man with a mass of unkempt dark gray hair wearing a white lab coat and black pants underneath. He's turned away from me, working at the island counter.

I clear my throat and he snaps around with a grimace and then he smiles.

"Oh, hello."

I smile nervously. "Hi. I'm Ash. I've been helping out here."

"Oh, right! Lisa told me you had started working already."

Chapter Ten

His face perks up and he gently sets the beakers he's holding down on the counter. Stepping toward me, he pulls off his latex gloves and extends his hand. "I'm Dr. Isaacs."

I shake his hand. "It's nice to finally meet you."

"And you as well," he says. "Lisa told me great things about you."

I look down to hide my red face. "That's very kind of her, but I'm not doing much."

"Nonsense, you've done quite a lot."

"It's only been one day."

"And you've already organized the supply cabinet," he says. "My career started right where you are, so I know how you're probably feeling, but I assure you, you're helping."

"Well, thank you for that." I move around the counter in an effort to get to work. Isaacs probably doesn't want to talk to me when he has work to—

"Do you have any interest in any of the sciences?"

I make a face. "Interest? Yes. Desire to pursue a career in science? No."

We both laugh.

"I get it," he says. "I just hope you appreciate its value."

"Oh absolutely," I say. "It's already proved its worth to me several times in my life." *My life* being confined to the last six weeks since I've been out of the cave.

"Much more than several, I assure you," he says. "It's fascinating what the earth has created—and continues to create—on its own. I love learning how science can use these creations to further develop unique substances that will only go on to help mankind."

"Wow, when you put it like that, it sounds exciting."

"Very exciting. Just think of all the medical advancements we've made in the last five, ten, fifteen years! Or even technology. From medical procedures to the sharing of information to the way we consume entertainment. Everything we do today is drastically different than how we did it fifty years ago. And it all started from materials that were available right here on our planet."

"Have you come up with anything that has had a big impact like that?"

"Well, I don't know if anything I've created has had *as* big of an impact, but I have developed some formulas that I believe could be life-changing."

"Like what?"

Dr. Isaacs looks up as he ponders. "Well, I concocted a solution that purified water. I thought it could be used by the missionaries in Africa to help clean the drinking water. Oh, and on another project, I developed a solution that could be consumed that would help the liver remove toxins from the body quicker."

"Really?" My excitement shows through with a big smile. "You did all that here?"

He nods. "Mm-hmm. I was never one to accept the idea that greatness can only be achieved in certain places. Opportunity is available everywhere. You'll see."

"Have you heard from the missionaries? Is the solution working? Or what about the one that clears the liver? How many people has that helped?"

He grumbles and looks down at his beakers again.

"Oh, I didn't mean to…" I trail off, wondering where this conversation went off course.

"Unfortunately, in the world we live in where money is more important than health, none of my inventions have been used outside of small experimental settings thanks to it taking so long to get approved by the FDA."

"Oh. That's a shame."

"And very frustrating," he adds.

"I can imagine." I indicate the beakers he's holding. Slowly, he pours the solution from one into the other. "What are you working on now?"

Chapter Ten

The interest in his work seems to brighten his mood again. "I won't bore you with the details, but after I successfully created a solution that could more quickly clear the toxins that were cycling through the liver, I developed a theory that would act in a similar manner. Only the intent wouldn't be to clear all toxins, but specific ones."

"Which ones?"

"Cancer."

My eyes perk up. "You're working on a cure for cancer?"

He shakes his head. "Not quite. What I'm hoping for is to simply slow the process at which cancer spreads so that patients can have a longer, more quality life."

"Any luck?"

Dr. Isaacs stirs the mixture. "I'm still looking for the right combination of solutions. If my calculations are correct, this should turn a faint blue, which would mean that one part of the compound is complete. Let's have a look."

After setting it on the counter, we both lower so we're eye-level with the beaker to avoid any obstructions. The mixture inside has the consistency of syrup.

"I don't see any blue," I say.

He groans. "Neither do I."

"Good morning." Lisa's voice pulls our attention away from his experiment. "Oh, I see you two have finally met."

I stand up straight. "Yeah, I got here early."

"Ash and I were just discussing some of my research," Dr. Isaacs tells her. "You're certainly here early as well."

She looks at her watch. "No, I'm right on time. Isn't your class starting now?"

He looks up at the clock. "Oh!" He turns to his desk, then turns back to the beaker.

"Leave it, I'll take care of it," I tell him.

"Thank you." He sets his safety glasses on his desk and pulls off his lab coat. "I apologize for rushing out like this. We'll continue our discussion later."

"Next time I see you."

He snatches up his briefcase from his desk and heads out the door.

———

AFTER WORK, I find myself at the Ellsworth Public Library again. Luckily this time, I'm sitting at a row of computers by myself. After talking to a librarian, who assisted me in finding the right databases to search, I'm finally ready to dig into my past.

The talk I had with Rachel last night made me realize that I'm the only one standing in my way of fully understanding my situation. I can't be afraid of what I might find because honestly, the stress about it is likely worse than what I'll actually discover.

Perry texted me and said he was unable to find me in EIT's database of alumni, so I'm looking through the library's index of yearbooks from Ellsworth City Schools. Since I'm probably in my twenties, the yearbooks are the next best bet since nothing came up at EIT. There are other colleges in the city but searching each and every one would take too long. The chances of me being a student in the public school system are higher. Hopefully it'll help me rediscover some of my friends, who will better be able to tell me about myself.

Still with my finger-pecks, I type my name into the database on the library's website. After I hit 'Enter' it brings up a list of search results:

"Ashton Cain, 1965"

"Ashton Cain, 1964"

"Ashton Cain, 1963"

"Ashton Cain, 1962"

"Well that can't be right…" I murmur to myself. Why would I be in a yearbook from the 60s? I do the math and figure that would probably line up more with Arlus's age. Since I know he's my brother, it's a start. I click on the top link.

The next page shows me the cover of the yearbook—a lion stenciled in reflective red ink with a cream background and the words "Ellsworth High School, 1965" written on the bottom—as well as a catalog listing.

Reaching for a scrap piece of paper, I write down the catalog numbers and go to the stacks of books to begin my search. At the back of the library, the last row of shelves hold old city records, oversized books, and yearbooks.

My fingers trail the weathered spines until I come across the yearbook from 1965. Pulling it out, I flip through the pages, finding the section devoted to the seniors. Since it's the most recent date listed, I'm assuming the 'Ashton Cain' I found on the database was a senior in 1965. Maybe he's my father. Maybe my real name is Ash Cain, Jr. Except, that would mean Arlus would be my uncle and he definitely confirmed that he was my brother.

I blink when I get to the correct page and study the picture for a while. How is this possible? The person staring back at me is…me. Almost exactly. Maybe a few years younger, but it's definitely the same person I see in the mirror every day.

But how? It has to be a mistake. It's 2019. I just saw it on the computer. It says so on the phone Perry got me. Not to mention, I look just as young as Rachel and Perry suspected. I *feel* as young as they say I am. There's no way that the person in this yearbook is me. There must be a mistake. Maybe this really is my father. But it doesn't make sense.

Still, I cling to that thought. It brings some relief to my panic and I plop down on the floor to look through the rest of the book in search of more answers about who this person was. *Hopefully* he's my father. He's shown in a picture with the soccer team as well as some other candids toward the end of the book from various school trips. In the candids, he's always with the same girl. Someone who looks very familiar to me. Almost…*intimately* familiar.

Dust Storm

Faint pieces of my memory return. How soft her skin felt. The way she giggled when I did something she thought was cute. The faint scent of coconut from her hair.

The thought that this might be my mother doesn't sit well with me. I have a gut feeling that she's *not* my mother. Not from the way I remember her. And if she's not my mother, then who is she? I know she's important to my life somehow. Why can't I remember who she is?

Flipping back to the senior portraits, I scan each student until I find hers. Linda Page.

My heart races as the familiarity turns to a series of flashbacks, like snapshots from my past. The glow of the lights at football games. Both of us dressed in fancy clothes and holding each other close. The way her hand fits easily into mine.

When I come out of it, I'm still hunched over the yearbook. Her picture stares up at me and I know. Linda is the girl from my flashbacks. The one from the courtyard at EIT. She's important to me.

Maybe she'll have answers or maybe she won't. I'll learn more about myself from the stories she can tell me then from what an internet search can. I need to find her.

Chapter Eleven

icking myself up from the mat, I make my way over to my bag in the corner. I'm breathing heavy and feeling sore, but mostly I feel energized. Another successful self-defense class.

I pull my water bottle out of my bag and guzzle half of it. If it wasn't for Tyrone already making it clear that it's not acceptable behavior for his gym, I'd squirt the rest of the bottle all over my head. Instead I stuff the bottle back into my bag. Nobody wants to push Tyrone on his rules.

"Good day?" Melissa reaches around me for her bag.

I step out of her way, watching my feet in the tangle of everyone else's belongings on the floor. "It was tiring, but good, yeah."

She smiles and slides her bag on her shoulder. "I noticed how you nailed that block. That was impressive."

"You were watching me?"

"I couldn't help but notice."

I return her smile. "You seem to be getting the hang of things too. Not that you came here as a complete novice."

She shrugs. "Meh, I had a good partner my first day here."

We start moving toward the stairs.

"Yeah? Is he a big guy?"

She scrunches her face. "Not really, but he's cute."

"Hey!"

Melissa laughs. "I'm kidding."

"Good!" I pat my bicep. "These guns are lethal."

She rolls her eyes. "Oh, I'm sure."

An awkward silence falls between us. Only the sound of our sneakers on the metal stair treads echo in the stairwell.

"Hey, are you in a rush to get anywhere?" she asks once we reach the bottom.

I shake my head. "Not really."

"Do you want to get coffee?" Her finger points to the café across the street.

Turning, I stare at the café as my mind spins. *No* is on the tip of my tongue, but I stop myself. After everything I've discovered at the library today, I want to get back to Rachel and Perry to fill them in. The memory of Linda fills my mind, but I push it away. She's filed with the things in my life marked "complicated." I told myself I wouldn't think about any of that until I talked it over with Rachel and Perry.

Besides, there's nothing wrong with Melissa. She makes me laugh. She's easy to talk to. The only thing holding me back is not knowing what to tell her about me, but I've skated around that before. I can do it again. There's nothing saying we're going to make this a habit after every class. Or maybe we will. I'll never know until I give it a shot.

Finally, I turn back to her. "Do you think they'll mind that we smell?"

Her fading smile lights back up again. "If they do, we know how to take them out."

"It's self-*defense*, not offense."

Chapter Eleven

She waves it off and looks up and down the street before crossing.

The café is in a small retail space carved out of a larger former warehouse, like the building we just had class in. Inside, there's exposed brick and ductwork. The lighting is dimmed in that coffee-space style and several plush pieces of furniture near the window are filled with laughing college students. It's only a few blocks from EIT.

Melissa and I order and take a seat at the small bar anchored along the brick wall. Knowing what I know now—or what I *think* I know—I wonder if I better belong in a time when these buildings were used for industry instead of retail.

I push away that thought. It's not the time for it right now. Besides, time travel is science fiction.

"So," I start.

"So," she echoes.

We both laugh anxiously.

"I'm sorry. I'm kind of nervous," I admit.

"Really? Why?"

I shrug. "I don't usually meet new people."

With two hands, Melissa grips the base of her coffee cup and studies it. "Well, I'm harmless." She flashes her big brown eyes at me. "Promise."

"Not from what I've seen in class."

She smiles. "That's a side of me that doesn't always get to show itself."

"Well, it's a feisty side."

"What about you? Right now you're just so *loud* and *intimidating* it's hard to take."

I shoot her a look at her sarcasm. "I'm not really shy, if that's what you're getting at."

She grins again. "So then tell me more about yourself."

"What do you want to know?"

"Are you working? Going to school? Have any siblings?

Where do you live? That sort of stuff." She makes a face and then puts up a hand to stop me. "Um. Not where you live. You don't have to answer that if you're not comfortable. I'm not going to, like, peek in your windows at night or anything."

I laugh. "It'd be pretty difficult. We're on the fifth floor."

"I like a challenge."

I consider the best way to move forward. I could lie and tell her that I'm taking classes at EIT, but that would catch up to me eventually if this post-class coffee thing becomes a habit. I could tell her the truth: that I'm working part-time cleaning a lab and doing nothing else while bumming on my friend's couch. That would make me sound pathetic. Instead, I try a different approach.

"To be honest, I'm having some memory issues."

Her smile fades and she sits up. "Oh my gosh, what happened?"

I shake my head. "It doesn't matter. Nothing horrible, that I can remember at least. I'm working with some people to try to get it all back, but it's a process."

Her bottom lip juts out a little. "That's so sad."

I take a sip of my coffee. "Yeah, it's not easy, but I'm working through it. Unfortunately, that means that I don't have a lot to offer in the way of conversation."

Realization crosses her face. "Oooh! That's why you hesitated when I asked you."

"Uh—yeah. Exactly."

"Don't worry, I'll tell you all about me," she says. "You just chime in whatever you can. Where should I start?"

"Uh, what about work? Or is it school?"

She shakes her head. "Work. I'm at Graybar Pharmaceuticals over on Willow Avenue." She points in the direction of her office.

"Oh that's different."

"Yeah, I've been there for a few years now. It's not bad."

"Any family?"

Chapter Eleven

"Just my parents. I'm an only child so I grew up a bit of a daddy's girl. Before I started working for Graybar, he actually wanted me to work for him doing the books for his construction business but it wasn't really for me."

"You gotta do what makes you happy."

She rolls her eyes and smirks. "I mean, pharmaceuticals isn't exactly my dream job, but it's not bad. I can find the happiness in it. And the paycheck reminds me of that happiness every two weeks."

We both laugh.

Melissa continues to take control of the rest of the conversation, telling me where she grew up and went to school. From the way she talks, I can tell she's someone who likes to help people and has very specific goals for herself, which is why she was disappointed when she failed out of her premed program.

After half an hour, I notice a familiar head of curly brown hair at the counter ordering a drink.

"Anyway, so I realized that I didn't have to be a doctor to help people," she goes on, not noticing my distraction. "A friend of mine suggested I started looking into options related to the medical field so my college credits wouldn't be a total waste and that's when I started drugs."

I try not to appear too distracted, but when the girl with the curls turns around, I know I have to say something.

"Ash?" Melissa asks. "Are you listening?"

I look at her and smile. "Huh? Yeah, I am."

"I just made a drug joke and you didn't even laugh. So either you're dead inside or you're not listening."

"Oh, sorry." Guess I wasn't being as discreet as I thought. "Actually, would you excuse me for a sec? I want to say hi to someone real quick."

She looks at me for a moment with big eyes, which I'm unable to read. "Oh. Okay. Sure. Go ahead."

"Sorry," I murmur and get up from my seat. Halfway across

the room, I kick myself for very clearly ditching Melissa like that. Especially to go talk to *another* girl. Guess I can probably rule out a second date.

"Sarah, hi."

She's standing at the counter with the cream and sugar. "Oh, hi."

"How are you doing?"

She shakes her head.

"Did you have any trouble taking time off?"

"No, it wasn't an issue." She secures the lid back on her coffee and says, "I'm sorry. I should probably go. My parents are going to worry if I'm gone too long. We're on our way back home."

"Oh, I'm sorry. I didn't mean to—"

On her way to the door she calls over her shoulder, "Don't worry about it."

"Wow, what was that about?" Melissa asks when I return to my seat.

I sigh and try think of the best way to explain it, but something doesn't sit well about the way she acted. Was she anxious to leave because she was afraid I was going to ask more questions about Abby? Did she tell the police that I was talking to her and now she feels guilty? Or is she guilty of something else entirely?

Duh, Ash, I tell myself. Her best friend was just murdered and nobody's found the killer yet. She's not likely to be very friendly at the moment.

My phone buzzes with a text from Perry.

"Where are you?" he asks.

"Who's that?" Melissa wonders.

"It's my roommate. I'm usually home by a certain time."

She picks up her empty cup and gets to her feet. "Well, we should get you home then." Any trace of joy is no longer present on her face.

I wonder if she's ending the date because she thinks I'm fragile with my memory loss or if she's mad that I said hi to Sarah.

At this moment, though—with Sarah still fresh on my mind—I'll take any excuse to get out of here. I can apologize, again, to Melissa later.

"Okay," I say in agreement. "I had a good time. I like talking to you."

She looks at me for a moment before a genuine smile emerges. "Should we do this again? After our next class?"

Apparently she's not too mad.

"I'd like that, yeah." I raise my phone up. "And I'll make sure he knows I'm going to be out later." I back into the door to hold it open for her, but stumble when it smacks into something—or rather, someone.

Turning, I look up at Dr. Isaacs. He glares at me.

I offer a friendly smile, but quickly wipe it away when I see his scowl.

"Watch where you're going," he says, apparently unaware that I'm his newest employee.

"Sorry." I step aside to allow him to pass and Barry enters right behind him.

"Hey, how are you?" he asks with a cheerful smile. At least *someone* recognizes me.

"Good."

He nods. "That's good to hear. Nice seeing you." Tapping me on the shoulder as he and Dr. Isaacs pass through, I can't help but wonder if he doesn't remember my name. Guess I can't blame him. I've only really talked to him a couple times.

Melissa follows me out onto the sidewalk. "Dr. Isaacs is such a grump," she says rather loudly. "I had him as a professor and I didn't like him from Day One."

"Come on, I'm sure he's not that bad. He was just annoyed. Maybe I accidentally hurt him or something."

"Or something," she mumbles.

We turn in the direction of the bus station.

"It was always obvious he hated teaching," she goes on.

"Refused to slow down, seemed annoyed when you asked questions, graded really hard. No wonder the students equally hated him."

Lisa *did* say that Dr. Isaacs mostly teaches so he could use the lab space, so Melissa's experience supports that idea. But you don't make a career doing something you hate. Even if it does come with perks. Dr. Isaacs must've enjoyed it at some point. Unless something was bothering him, causing stress that ricocheted to other aspects of his life.

I clear my throat. "Oh, I kind of work for him now—"

As we walk by the alley between buildings, our happy evening goes grim as the wind picks up, pulling at our hair and clothes, sending a chill straight to the core. The sound intensifies as sand arrives from somewhere above us, bouncing off of me, growing with intensity until my skin starts to chafe from the tiny abrasions.

I shut my eyes tight as Melissa screams beside me, presumably taking the same instinctual defensive measures as me. My heart pounds in my chest. Is this what killed Mitch and Abby? How am I supposed to fight it if I can't even open my eyes? Worse, since I came from self-defense, it's one of the rare times I don't have my Heat suit on under my clothes.

I stumble backward in an effort to get out of the storm and to my surprise, a few steps away, the wind and the sand stop smacking my face. Like night and day.

But Melissa still screams.

Quickly wiping the sand out of my eyes, I open them and see that she's still trapped in the cyclone. There's no one around directing the sand. No physical aspect of it except for the storm. I don't even know where to direct my attack.

Melissa's screams stifle as a steady stream of sand flies into her open mouth.

Without thinking, my fists ignite into flame and I shoot a stream of fire at the center of the twister, careful not to get too close to Melissa.

Chapter Eleven

The heat from the flame does the trick and the sandstorm raises into the sky and flies away, leaving Melissa on all fours on the sidewalk coughing up sand.

I rush to her. "Are you okay?"

She's gasping for air, but coughing is a good sign that at least *something's* getting through to her lungs.

Pulling out my phone, I call 9-1-1 and hope that she's able to get to the hospital in time to save her.

Chapter Twelve

ow's she doing?" Perry asks later in the emergency waiting room.

I shrug. "No idea. Rachel went in to check a while ago. I really hope she's okay."

"And you're sure it was this…dust cloud."

"Definitely. It didn't seem like someone threw an attack so much as it was…its own being. Like someone *became* the cloud."

"Dust Storm!" he blurts. "That's a better name. Forget I said the other one."

"Perry, this is serious," I tell him. "What if Melissa dies only because she was in the wrong place at the wrong time?"

He opens his mouth to respond, but Rachel walks through the doors from the rest of the hospital.

I stand and meet her halfway. "How's she doing?"

Perry comes up beside us.

"She'll be fine," she starts. "It's just going to take a while. She breathed in a lot of sand, but not enough to cause any permanent damage. The doctors are giving her fluids to help wash it all out. One solution in particular will help coat the lining of her throat to help ease the pain, but it's still going to hurt."

"Sounds like it," Perry adds.

"Yeah. It's essentially like rubbing sandpaper all along the inside of her windpipe and esophagus," she says.

I put both of my hands on the top of my head and look up at the ceiling. "That's horrible. This is all my fault."

There's a momentary pause between my friends.

"Why don't we sit down somewhere?" Rachel suggests. "Maybe get a coffee or something."

I shake my head. "No, I want to see her when I can."

She nods. "You will. But it's still going to be a while. They haven't given her a room yet and until they do, only family and hospital staff are allowed back there. I have a friend who is an ER nurse. She said she'd let me know when Melissa's being moved. Until then, there's no point in just sitting around and wallowing in pity. Let's go somewhere to talk."

Perry puts a hand on my back and starts to lead me down the hall toward the hospital cafeteria. "Come on. We can sit somewhere quieter."

The cafeteria is just as crowded as the ER, but it is certainly quieter. I take a seat at a table in the corner while Rachel and Perry go up and get something from the counter. He comes back with two cookies and she has a cup of coffee in her hand.

"Here, it's chocolate chip." Perry sets the extra cookie on a napkin on the table and takes the seat across from me.

I ignore it and stare off into nothingness.

"Ash, she's going to be okay," Rachel says. "Actually, she's lucky because in all reality, she didn't consume that much sand. If she would've taken much more we'd be having an entirely different conversation."

"Yeah." I stare out the window at the city lights. Saying that Melissa is 'lucky' doesn't make me feel any better. She was attacked, completely unprovoked. More importantly, she was attacked in likely the same manner as Mitch and Abby were. Which means someone in that cafe had a connection to not only the EIT campus, but to all three victims.

My mind goes right to Sarah. She left shortly before Melissa and I did and she seemed very standoffish with me. Not only that, but she was best friends with Abby and knew Mitch as well. Plus, Sarah was the only one around when Abby died.

But with all of those pieces of the puzzle linking her to the crime, I can't figure out what her motive was. Or is, since Dust Storm is still attacking. Why would she kill her best friend and her neighbor? And would she really be able to fake the kind of remorse I saw in her? And what is her connection to Melissa?

Of course, we also saw Dr. Isaacs and Barry at the café. Isaacs seemed agitated and I can't remember how Barry was. The fact that they were even together is weird. Sure, their labs are right next to each other, but neither of them, nor anyone else, have ever mentioned them being friends.

The other question is how could someone from inside a crowded café sneak out and attack us within minutes of me and Melissa leaving? Why would they want to? And if this Dust Storm really is a person, how did they get their powers?

"What are you thinking?" Rachel breaks into my thoughts.

I sigh. "I'm thinking we found our killer."

"A swarm of dust?"

"Dust Storm," Perry corrects her.

She looks at him over her cup. "You're really not giving up on this naming thing, are you?"

"Not if I can help it."

She rolls her eyes and turns back to me. "So you just need to find out who turned into…Dust Storm…"

Perry winks and shoots a finger gun her way.

"Yeah," I murmur.

"How do you even know that cloud is a person?" she asks.

Chapter Twelve

"Maybe it's just an attack."

I shake my head. "No, we went over this. The cloud—Dust Storm—seemed to attack with purpose. It's not like we could've dodged it or anything."

"But a person turning into a million tiny pieces of sand? That sounds a little far-fetched. Even for what we've seen."

"Not necessarily," Perry tells her. "Ash can essentially turn to flame when he flies, so in theory Dust Storm's DNA could've been altered so much that he doesn't need to maintain a physical body."

"And," I add, "we haven't heard about the police moving in on a suspect, which means that they can't figure it out either."

"That could just mean that they haven't found enough proof to arrest someone yet," she says.

"Maybe so, but based on our other theories about this guy, we're going to have to assume that the cloud is Dust Storm," I say. "If we keep waiting for more answers then more people are going to get hurt."

She nods slowly for a moment. "You're right. But you're still basically saying that you don't know who killed them."

"Not technically," I say, "but we know that it was someone who could change their shape, not just *throw* the sand."

"I guess that helps." She takes a sip.

"Any theories on the suspect?" Perry asks.

I nod. "You're not going to like them."

"Who?"

"Uh…let's just say they're employees that you've had contact with," I say vaguely.

"And so did the victims," Rachel adds. "Are they researchers?"

I nod again.

"If you want to tell *me* their names, I can see what I can dig up on their professional backgrounds," she offers.

"Seriously!" he blurts. "You're not going to tell me?"

"I will," I say. "Just not right now."

"Why not?" he pushes.

"Because I have something else to tell you," I say. "Both of you."

Rachel furrows her brow. "What is it?"

"Does it have anything to do with Dust Storm?" he asks.

"No."

"Really?" she asks. "You've been consumed with all this investigation stuff lately."

"I know, but this is big too," I say.

Frankly, I could also use the distraction. Not that what I'm about to tell them is really an escape from reality at all.

Perry snatches up the cookie he got for me. "Is this about your past?"

I nod. "I found something…weird."

"Weird how?" she asks.

"Well, I was at the library and got on this yearbook index search thing," I start.

"Oh, so you actually listened to me?" she says with a smirk.

I shoot her a look and go on. "The only yearbooks that had my name in them were from the 1960s."

"The 60s?" he blurts. "Are you sure you were searching the right thing?"

"Positive," I say. "I pulled the yearbook and I found a picture of…me—or someone who looks like me. I don't know."

Rachel and Perry exchange glances.

Sensing the skepticism, I pull out my phone and show them the pictures I took of the yearbook.

"Are you sure this isn't your father?" Perry hands me back my phone. "Maybe you're a junior or the third or something like that."

"That's what I thought too, but then I found this." I swipe to the next picture and hand it back to him.

He shrugs. "You and some girl?"

"Linda Page. That's the girl from my visions." I pass the phone over to Rachel.

"You're sure?" Her fingers pinch at the screen to zoom in.

I nod. "Positive. I don't know how it's possible. I *vividly* remember her." I clear my throat to buy time. "*Personal* things."

"Okay, okay, okay," Rachel rattles off. "We get it." She hands me back my phone.

"So you're saying this Linda girl is your girlfriend?"

I shrug. "That's what we've been assuming."

They're quiet as they both consider it.

"I mean, I guess it kind of lines up with Arlus being your brother," Perry finally says.

"How?" Rachel asks.

"Think of the timeframe," he explains. "Those photos are in a yearbook from the 60s."

"The last one was 1965," I clarify.

"And if Ash and Arlus are brothers and Arlus is in his seventies, that would mean he was born sometime in the 40s and would likely be around high school age in the 60s."

Rachel gestures to me. "But *look* at him. Ash is not in his seventies. So how does any of this add up?"

I shrug. "Maybe it's all an elaborate hoax set up by Arlus to get me to trust him or something."

"But why?" she asks.

"I don't know. Maybe his power also allows him to alter photos or memories or something. I very much doubt that we saw the extent of his power."

"That's scary," Perry mutters.

"Yeah," I say. "But I did some more digging and found where Linda lives now—"

"Nope, bad idea," Rachel interrupts.

"Why?"

"Ash, *something* happened," she says. "There's a reason you look like you're twenty when you're supposedly seventy."

"I agree," Perry adds. "When Linda sees you, she's going to flip out or think she's going senile or something. Somehow you disappeared for fifty years—*if* this story is actually accurate. Don't you think Linda's going to question that?"

"Yeah, I guess," I admit. "But I think talking to Linda is the fastest way to learn everything about me. If Arlus is somehow altering my past, hopefully Linda can tell me what *really* happened."

"Unless it involves her too," she says.

"That's a chance I'm going to have to take," I counter.

Rachel shakes her head but doesn't add anything else.

"Ash, it's an option that we can consider after we've exhausted the others," Perry says. "Until then, I think you should wait. Try looking through old newspaper headlines or missing persons reports. If you disappeared, there should be some documentation of that."

"Unless Arlus destroyed all of that," I say. "If this *is* an elaborate hoax by him, then that documentation would be the first things to go."

"It's a start," Rachel says.

"Who knows?" Perry adds. "By going to see her, you might be putting a target on her back that would lead Arlus right to her. Staying away from her could be for her protection."

"And there are other ways you can find out who you are," she adds. "You just need to be careful. That's all we're saying. Talking to Linda sounds like a risk. For both of you."

I sigh. It's hard to ignore the most promising lead to my past, but my friends make some good points. I don't want Linda to be in danger. But aren't I just keeping myself in danger by staying ignorant? If I knew the story—no matter how horrible—maybe I could piece together the Gatekeeper's grudge against me. Maybe even find a way to stop him.

"Okay, I'll wait," I tell them.

It's a promise I don't plan on keeping. Linda and I shared

Chapter Twelve

an intense bond—maybe even fifty years ago. I know she'd be happy to see me, no matter how different we are now. Besides, now that I've found some answers about my past, I can't stop the hunt now.

Chapter Thirteen

Y ou're an idiot," Perry says into my comm.

"It's the best idea I've been able to come up with." I'm standing on the roof of the Herbert building in my Heat suit, overlooking the nearest parking lot and the walkways below. I've been here since four in the morning waiting for Dust Storm to show up.

"I think the chances of you stumbling on the murderer are pretty slim," he adds. "I can't imagine he travels in that cyclone—although I suppose that *would* save time and money, not to mention it's really cool."

I walk along the edge of the roof, scanning the ground below. No sign of anything suspicious. A few early birds, but no one else. "Well, the first two attacks happened right here on campus and the third happened at a place where a lot of students frequent, so Dust Storm must be going after students."

"Melissa isn't a student."

"All right, maybe not *students* specifically, but he's connected to EIT somehow." I didn't get the chance to see her last night. They moved her into her own room after visiting hours were over, but Rachel went up to check and said she's doing fine. Still, it would've been nice to see her myself.

"Okay, so let's say you do find Dust Storm," he says. "How are you going to stop him?"

"He seemed to retreat when I threw fire at him last time," I reply. "Maybe he has an aversion to heat?"

"Maybe. It still seems like it's a long shot."

"Isn't glass made up of melted sand?" I glance down at a security guard strolling along the walkway. "Couldn't I just crank up the heat until he turns into a window?"

"In theory, yeah, but unless you can get him into an insulated room that would contain the heat, you'd have a hard time reaching a temperature that high," he says. "And that's if you're even *able* to reach a temperature that hot."

"How hot?"

Through the earpiece, I hear fingers clacking on a keyboard. "Uh…" He chuckles. "Three thousand, ninety degrees Fahrenheit sustained for *at least* ten minutes."

"Damn."

"Exactly. So good idea, but not very feasible."

"Maybe it'll at least slow him down."

"I really don't think so," he says. "Not in an open environment. Your time is probably better spent figuring out how he *became* Dust Storm and trying to counteract that. Approach him as a person instead of a super."

"I don't know how he became Dust Storm!" My words carry across campus and I slink away from the edge to hide. I lower my voice before I continue, "I barely know anything about *my* powers, let alone someone I've only encountered once."

"It was just a thought," he says. "Either way, you need a better plan."

"Do you have any ideas?"

He's quiet. "Actually, I might."

"Like what?" Moving along the perimeter of the building, I check the other entrances to make sure nobody's sneaking by. Then again, I have no one watching the tunnels, so this really is a wasted trip. The attack on Melissa keeps replaying in my head. At least now I'm doing *something* to stop Dust Storm.

"Well, while I was between jobs I started working on a prototype for a device that would essentially dampen energy in whoever was wearing it."

"Dampen their energy?"

"Almost like a sedative, only for people like you and Dust Storm, since you have extra abilities. I believe that it would actually dampen your powers."

"How?"

"A variation on chelation therapy that's instant and takes effect with skin contact."

"*What* therapy?"

"Chelation. It's used to treat extreme mercury poisoning, which, as we've found out, mercury is how you have your powers," he explains. "It's still a prototype, especially since I'm working on theory here. We *assume* the mercury is only in your blood, not in the rest of your organs. And we also *assume* that Dust Storm's powers are a result of the same exposure. If this device works, Dust Storm will be without his powers—or rather, his powers will be considerably weakened—when he's wearing it."

"Oh, so you're saying that if I get Dust Storm back to his human form and get this device on him, he won't be able to turn back into the cyclone?"

"Yeah, exactly. It's still a very rough prototype. I wanted to have something for when you faced off against the Gatekeeper again, but with two people dead and another one in the hospital, stopping Dust Storm takes precedence."

"Where is it? Do you have it?"

"It's in my lab over there."

"Perfect, I'll go grab it." I head over to the door to the staircase leading downstairs.

"Ash, I'm not positive it's going to work," he says quickly. "I wouldn't rely on it. There are still a lot of unknowns."

"I trust you."

"Yeah, well for this device, I'm not sure *I* trust myself. If you get in contact with it, *you* could lose your powers."

"It'll be fine, Perr. Don't worry."

The building is still mostly empty when I get inside, but I know that'll change soon. In the meantime, at least I know that no one will see me in my suit. The last thing I need is the media here to try to get new footage of Heat.

At the top of the stairs leading down to the basement I hear loud voices, but I can't make out what they're saying. Stepping lightly, I continue down and slip behind the stairs for cover, straining to make out who they are and what they're talking about.

"I'm backing out!"

Definitely someone who's younger. Not a student, though. Maybe early thirties, if that.

"You can't back out!"

Unmistakably, that's Dr. Isaacs.

"This isn't what I signed up for."

Wait, I know that voice. Is that…?

The conversation quiets, but without the sound of movement I know it's not over. Do they know I'm here? If it were just Dr. Isaacs, I could sneak into Perry's lab undetected but I can't risk it with more eyes to potentially spot me. Of course, I could also come back later as Ash, but how many more people would get hurt then? Would he go after Melissa again? I still haven't figured out Dust Storm's motive yet.

Still hiding behind the corner, I hear footsteps coming down the hall. A moment later, Barry walks out with his eyes glued to his phone. Good thing, too, because from beneath the open metal staircase, he definitely would've seen me if he didn't have a distraction.

Once he's out of sight, I creep into Perry's lab and scan over his desk. Among the various papers, folders, and used to-go containers sits half a dozen gadgets and tools.

"Which one is it?" I whisper into the comm.

"Should be one of the little ones. Looks almost like a watch or a bracelet."

I pick up the only one that matches that description and study it to make sure I have the right one. The wristband is made up of a fabric that's almost like seatbelt material. Attached to that is a small plastic chamber that looks like a battery pack. I describe it to Perry, who confirms I've got the right thing.

"All right, now get out of there before anyone sees you and thinks Heat is stealing stuff," he tells me, then grumbles, "You could've just waited until I went in later this morning…"

Clutching the device in my fist, I step toward the door. "No, I want to have it in case—"

The sound of pitter-pattering sand grows like a rising crescendo until it nearly becomes deafening. In front of me, the cyclone that is Dust Storm appears in the doorway, forcing me further back into the room. With the increased wind, the door slams shut, leaving me trapped inside.

"Never mind, I'm going to need a crash course on how this thing works." I back away until I hit a desk, then slide sideways, trying to keep my distance.

"Why? What's going on?" Perry asks in my ear.

"How does this thing work!?" I duck to the floor as a stream of dust lunges at me and splatters against the brick wall, retaking its shape in the air moments later.

"Okay, there's a switch on the side. Flick it and a red light should turn on."

Not taking my eyes off the cyclone, I feel for the switch on the device and turn it on. Out of the corner of my eye, I think I catch a glimpse of a red light.

"Now what?"

"Put it on him," he says.

"How am I supposed to do that?"

Dust Storm attacks again and I dive to the left, ducking behind the center island for cover.

"This comm lets me be your ears, not your eyes," he says. "I've never even seen Dust Storm before!"

"It doesn't have a body!" Maybe if I can get it to revert back to its physical form by using my fire power on it, that'll give me enough time to strap Perry's device on it.

I run the length of the small room and head toward the door, but Dust Storm is too fast and wraps me in its swirl. Shutting my eyes and mouth tight to keep any sand from slipping through, I raise my hands to plug my ears and feel the device slip away.

"What's going on?" Perry panics in my ear. "All I'm getting is static!"

Just like with Melissa, I feel the swarm of sand close in on me further and further. Particles work its way through the fabric of my suit and rattle against my face, trying to gain access inside to kill.

I have to do something. I can't let this stupid weather system get the better of me. Images of Melissa's attack flash in my mind. Namely, how I got Dust Storm to back off. Gathering my rage, I wait until the sand is almost too much to bear and then let my entire body erupt.

Immediately, the sand pulls away from me, sending papers and gadgets in the room flying and leaving scorch marks nearby. The sand regathers and slips through the cracks around the door and out of the room, leaving silence in its wake.

My comm explodes with Perry's roar, "What the hell is going on!?"

Chapter Fourteen

"Good morning, Ash," Dr. Isaacs says later when I arrive for work.

"Morning." I come around the other side of the island counter and pause. After the attack in Perry's lab, I went back to his apartment and explained what happened. He told me to try to get some answers out of both Isaacs and Barry. Hence, why I'm here early.

Dr. Isaacs looks up. "Is there something the matter?"

"No—well, maybe. Sort of."

He chuckles. "That's not very definitive."

"Sorry." I motion over to Perry's lab. "My friend said he found some sand next door when he came in this morning. The same kind of sand that was found when that student died."

"Sand?" Dr. Isaacs repeats. "That's strange."

I ignore him. "There was sand in the staircase of the Main Hall where the other student was killed too."

"Interesting."

Chapter Fourteen

"Yeah. So it's pretty likely that whoever killed them was also in my friend's lab either last night or this morning," I go on. "I talked to a janitor and he said the room was cleaned last night, so it must've happened this morning."

"Ash, what are you suggesting?"

"I know you get here early to work on your research before your classes, did you notice anything when you came in?"

He looks off toward the door. "No, I didn't. And, as I've told the police, I actually wasn't here early the day the student was found."

"Where were you?"

He thinks. "Stuck in traffic. I live on the south side of the city and I-23 was backed up due to an accident."

"What time do you normally get in?"

"Why are you asking me these questions?"

"*What time?*" I push.

He lets out a deep breath. "Around seven. The day the student was found, I was actually late for class, so I got here sometime after eight."

I make a mental note to check his alibi.

Stepping over to his desk, he closes his briefcase and turns back to me. "Speaking of class, I should get going to mine. That is, unless you have more suggestive questions for me?"

I shake my head.

"Well then, good day, Ash."

We stare at each other as he crosses the room and disappears out the door.

―――

"I DON'T LIKE it," Perry tells me after I'm done with work. We're in the cafeteria finishing lunch. I've just told him about my encounter with Isaacs this morning.

"Neither do I," I tell him.

"I think he's lying. Or hiding something. Or covering for someone."

"I still have to look into his story to verify it," I say. "But there were two people in the basement this morning."

He shakes his head, knowing who I mean. "Barry didn't kill them."

"Perry, you don't know that for sure. The way he and Isaacs were arguing this morning—"

"So are you going to confront him the same way you did Isaacs? Cause that didn't work out the way you wanted it to."

"Well, I'm hoping it'll go smoother this time, but yeah. I have to talk to him."

He sighs heavily and stares at me. "Why? Aren't there any other leads you can track down?"

"I tried. Mitch doesn't have any exes, from what I can tell. Neither his nor Abby's roommates have anything questionable about them. And both of them were freshmen so it's not like they had any grudges with any other students. With the police confiscating their computers and phones, it's not like I can really look around for anything on there. As of right now, the most promising leads we have are Murphy and Isaacs."

"Oh, so it's last-names-only now?"

"Perry, Murphy is suspicious," I say. "I didn't want to tell you this, but one of the janitors saw Mitch and Barry arguing a few days before Mitch died."

"So?"

"So? Perry, depending on what they were arguing about, that could be Barry's motive."

"Or it could be something else."

"I don't think it was," I push.

"You can't just go around accusing people, Ash."

"I know, but—" I stop myself before this disagreement escalates. "What does Barry research? What's his specialty?"

"Uh…rocks. Geology and stuff."

"What was he working on specifically?"

"I don't know, Ash," he says. "Even though we all share a lab, we only really have a passing interest in each other's work. Besides, I'm still new."

"But it's possible that Barry could've been working with rocks taken from the cave I woke up in?"

Perry narrows his eyes. "I don't think Barry is Dust Storm."

"Maybe not, but we won't know until we get some more answers. We need to talk to him, Perr."

"When?"

"The sooner the better."

He crinkles up his trash into his fist and sighs heavily. "All right then. Come on. He should be finishing with lunch anytime now."

Surprised by his sudden change of tone, I hurry to catch up to him.

We head back to Herbert. Neither of us say anything. The fact that I'm even considering a colleague of Perry's—likely now a friend to him—creates a noticeable uncomfortableness between us. Hopefully Barry's story will not only make sense, but check out too. Although if Barry's story eliminates him as a suspect, that leaves my main suspect to be Isaacs.

"Hey, Barr, you have a minute?" Perry asks once we're back in his lab.

The rest of their coworkers are seated at their desks working, the scent of their lunches still lingering. The previous night's leftovers create a delicious aroma that makes me wonder if I should eat anything else for lunch. None of them look up when we enter. They're too busy with their work.

Barry turns to us. "Yeah, what's up?"

Perry nods out into the hall. "Let's go for a walk."

He follows us out and up the stairs.

"You remember my friend Ash, right?"

"Yeah, how's it going?" Barry shakes my head and offers a smile.

"Good." I don't offer anything else. I'm not sure if Perry

wants to be the one to lead the conversation. I wasn't expecting him to even be in the conversation, but I guess it's probably better this way. If Barry is involved, he'll be less defensive with Perry asking the questions than me.

"You're working for Isaacs, right?" Barry asks as we follow Perry out of the building.

I nod. "Cleaning the lab. So not as impressive as what you guys are doing."

"Hey, you're still getting paid."

"That's true."

Perry leads us toward the courtyard. The sky is gloomy, so there aren't many students laying out in the grass today. Which is good, because we don't need anyone overhearing us. It's probably why Perry led us out here to begin with.

"So what's up?" Barry slides his hands in his pockets and leans against the trunk of a tree in the courtyard.

Perry looks at me, waiting for me to start.

"I saw you and Dr. Isaacs at the coffee shop on Chestnut Avenue last night," I say.

His eyes light up. "Oh! That was you! Sorry, I thought I knew you from somewhere, but I couldn't place you. It must've just been a different setting."

"Don't worry about it." I cross my arms. "So you and Isaacs are friends then?"

He shrugs. "Yeah, I guess so."

"You guess so?" Perry asks.

"Well, our labs are right next to each other and we come in around the same time so we've chatted a few times."

"Must've been more than a few times if you went to get coffee after hours," Perry says.

Barry smirks. "You're still new. After a while you'll get the office etiquette. Sometimes we just like to get together and talk about our research. To people who understand what we're talking about. Explaining it to the wife every day gets tiring."

Chapter Fourteen

"Is that what you were arguing about this morning before the rest of your colleagues arrived?" I ask.

Barry blinks.

"And what's weird is that when I said good morning to Charlie today, he asked me if all of my co-workers were okay," Perry adds. "I guess he thought that there was another attack because there was sand all over the office, just like there was when Mitch Mantel died."

"Guys, you're way off base here." He puts up his hands and tries to sneak around the tree. "I have no idea how the sand got there. And I really don't think that has anything to do with the murder. Why? Did you hear something from the police?"

"Never mind the police for right now." I step forward and he backs flat against the tree trunk. "Let's talk about that argument you had with Mitch a few days before he died."

"Does every argument need to be scrutinized?" he asks.

"I guess not. Perry tells me you're a researcher?"

Barry looks over to my friend and then back to me. "Yeah. Geology. I'm working on a soil study right now."

"So you're not a professor?"

"No, what are you getting at?"

"I'm just trying to understand why someone whose job doesn't require him to have any real contact with students had an argument with one several days before he died," I say. "You didn't have any sort of relationship with Mitch outside of—"

"That is *not* what's going on here." Barry points his finger in my direction. "I'm not some pervert preying on innocent kids."

"Then what else would you two be arguing about?"

Barry grits his teeth, but doesn't offer anything.

"Okay, well if you won't answer that, maybe you could tell me where you were the night Mitch Mantel was murdered because I gotta tell you, it's more than a little suspicious that he died cleaning *your* lab and *you* were the one who found him the next morning, especially after what we just discussed. And Perry tells me you're usually the last one to leave at night. So unless you tell me where you were that night, I'm going to have to assume that you were—"

"I was at the gym!" he blurts.

"Which gym?" Perry asks.

"Planet Fitness on Maple."

"And Isaacs? Where was he?" I ask.

He shrugs again. "I don't know! You're going to have to ask him."

"So what were you arguing about this morning?" I push.

"Business stuff," he says. "We have a shared investment. Something that *he* controls."

So clearly they're pretty good friends if they both put money toward something.

"Stocks?" Perry asks.

He shakes his head. "No, but just as risky."

"Like what?" I ask.

Barry stares at me with a hard expression. "Look. I gave you my story. I told you where I was when that kid died. I don't know how the sand got into the lab this morning—maybe it was a prank. There are rumors all over campus. But I don't need to disclose *all* of my personal details. You're not cops. Besides, *I'm* not the only one who works in that lab, *Perry*."

I look over at Perry and know that he's thinking the same thing: Barry's right. We're toeing the line here and if we push it much further, there will be consequences for us. Maybe even Perry's job.

"Okay," I say after a few seconds. "We're just trying to help figure all of this out."

"It's horrible what happened to that student," he says. "But you need to believe me when I say: *I didn't kill him.*"

"Yeah, of course." Perry pats him on the shoulder but Barry shrugs it off. "We just need to be sure."

My phone starts buzzing in my pocket. I pull it out and see

Chapter Fourteen

Sarah Sanders' name displayed across it. "Hey, I'll catch up with you guys later."

They walk off back toward Herbert and leave me standing in the courtyard under the cover of the trees. Sliding my finger across my screen, I answer the call.

"Hello?"

"Hey, uh, Ash?" Her voice sounds small, almost nervous.

"Sarah? What's going on? Did something happen?"

"No, but I remembered some more stuff I thought might be helpful," she says. "You told me to call you if I thought of anything."

"Yeah, of course!" Hopefully this will help shape up the theory we're putting together. Still, it's kind of strange that she ignored me yesterday when I saw her in the café with Melissa and today she's calling me with more information.

"I'd rather not do it over the phone," she says. "Could you meet me somewhere? Maybe at the bench outside the dorm at EIT, where we talked before?"

"Sure, I'm actually right in the courtyard," I say. "You want to talk now?"

There's a pause and then she says, "Yeah, now works. See you in a bit."

Sliding my phone back in my pocket, I head over to the bench and take a seat. I try not to stare at the door as I wait, but I can't help it. Every time it swings open, I look up to see if it's Sarah. I wonder what she has to say. She seemed to cover it all the last time we talked. But that was also right after Abby died. Maybe she has a theory as to why Dust Storm would want her dead. Anything could help at this point.

Several minutes later, when the door opens my heart drops and I realize I've been tricked. Detective Jenna Harkness steps out and approaches me.

"Ashton Cain—if that is your name—I think we need to have a chat."

Chapter Fifteen

Keeping my eyes low to avoid my reflection in the two-way mirror, I study my hands. I'm sitting at the only table in the room, waiting for Detective Harkness to return. She's been gone a long time, probably so I start to feel nervous and spill any details I might otherwise try to hide.

It's working.

Just like Rachel warned against, I've been sticking my nose into this investigation since the beginning. If anything, I'm surprised they haven't brought me in sooner.

I can't help but feel a little betrayed by Sarah, but I guess I can't really blame her. To her, I probably looked like a creep so desperate for gossip that I'd interrogate a girl just after she found her best friend dead. Even I have to admit it sounds suspicious.

Leaning forward, I bury my face in my hands. This is a mess. Getting in trouble with the police was definitely *not* on my agenda, but here we are. I rub my eyes with the heels of my hands. This is a nightmare.

Chapter Fifteen

The door opens and my head snaps up.

"Not feeling well, Mr. Cain?" Harkness comes around the table and places a manila folder down in front of me. She sets her one hand on her hip and the other leaning on the table over the folder she just set down. "Imagine how Sarah Sanders felt right after her friend died."

"That was a misunderstanding—"

"Oh, trust me, I want to hear how you explain yourself out of this one, but first we need to talk about a few other things."

I look down at my hands again.

Harkness takes the seat across from me and folds her hands. "Sarah said you were asking her some personal questions. What she saw when Abby died, who might've wanted to harm her—"

"I was only trying to help."

"So then why not come to us with that information?" she asks. "We already talked to you at the crime scene. Seems to me like that was the perfect moment to say whatever you had on your mind. Better yet, you could've just left it up to us. That is what most people do. So why were you so interested?"

There's no way I can answer that honestly, so I just shrug.

She flips open the folder and pulls out two sheets. One from the notepad she had when she interviewed me at the crime scene in the Main Hall and another a printout from a computer.

Tapping the notepad paper she asks, "This is your number, correct? The one you gave me the last time we talked?"

I glance at it and nod. "Yeah."

She slides the computer paper toward me. "These are Mitch Mantel's phone records. Is there a reason you were calling and texting him the day after his death?"

I swallow hard, but don't offer an explanation.

"If you take a look at those time stamps, it was *after* Abby was killed too." She studies me, but I remain silent. Sitting up, she opens her jacket and pulls out a cell phone from an inside pocket, fumbling with the screen for a bit. Finally, she sets it in front of me and the message I left for Mitch plays.

"Hi Mitch. My name is Ash. I have some news about a friend of yours. Please call me ASAP."

"Abby's death was just an excuse, wasn't it?"

Still, I don't say anything. Don't even look at her. My mind is spinning as I stare at the hard evidence right in front of me. It's what might even get me arrested for interfering with an investigation. Maybe worse.

"You realize it's highly suspicious that you have connections to both crime scenes, right?"

I nod.

"Did you know the victims?"

I shake my head.

"Neither of them?"

"No." Through my fear, the word comes out as a croak.

"So then why were you getting involved?"

Silence.

Harkness collects the papers back in the folder and leans back in her chair with her arms folded. "Who are you?"

My brow furrows and I look up. "My name's Ash."

"You're going to stick with that?"

Doing my best to feign confusion instead of panic, I stutter, "I—I don't—"

She opens the folder again and pulls out another computer sheet and sets it in front of me. It's a copy of a driver's license issued in 1963. Very similar to the picture I showed Rachel and Perry from the yearbook.

"This is the only record of Ashton Cain that I could find." She taps her finger to the picture. "This guy disappeared in 1969."

I stare up at her incredulously. "What?"

"What's your real name?"

Ignoring her, I look down and study the picture more. Aggravated, she pulls it away.

"Answer the question."

Chapter Fifteen

"I don't understand," I tell her. "I've been having some memory problems."

"Convenient," she mutters.

"I'm telling the truth," I push. "I know my name is Ash Cain, but beyond that, I don't know much else about myself."

Sitting back and crossing her arms again, Harkness looks at me with disbelief.

"It's the truth," I repeat.

Shaking her head, she gets to her feet. "No, actually. I don't believe it is. What you're saying doesn't make sense. The *only* Ash Cain on file is this one and unless you can explain how you disappeared for fifty years, I don't believe you."

The cave.

The Gatekeeper.

Arlus.

She gathers up the papers in her folder and steps to the door. "Unless you're ready to tell me the real story, I've got better things to do." She lingers, waiting for my response, but when one doesn't come she rolls her eyes and walks out.

———

"YOU'RE WHERE?" RACHEL asks me over the phone an hour later. It's my one phone call. Figured it'd be better to reach out to her instead of Perry. He'd probably still be at work and it would run the risk of Barry overhearing.

"I'm at the police station," I tell her. "I think they think I'm a suspect."

"On what grounds?"

"Interference," I mutter, painfully aware of the uniform standing beside me.

"Ash, I *told* you!"

"I know! I know! Could you save the lecture for when I'm not freaking out?"

She sighs. "Sorry. What do you need me to do?"

"Help get me out of here, that would be nice."

"I'll try to think of something. How did they even book you?" she asks. "You don't have any of your papers or anything."

"Yeah, that's another thing the detective was asking me about. She pulled my license from the 60s."

"Tell her to join the club."

"That's not going to go over very well. I haven't officially been arrested yet, but when I can't offer a better excuse for the license, arrest is probably inevitable."

She sighs. "I'll think of something."

"Thanks."

"Hey, before you go there's something I need to tell you," she says. "It actually might help exonerate you if you can point to another person who did the crime."

"But the person who did it is—"

"Dust Storm, I know. But after the fires the Gatekeeper spread across the city a couple months ago and, you know, *Heat* being a presence in the city, then putting the blame rightfully on Dust Storm might not be too far of a stretch."

"That's a big maybe."

"Just hear me out. I've been looking through some of the medical journals I could find online to refresh my memory of what I read about Dr. Isaacs and his treatments."

"And?"

"Well, his research for this one case makes sense in theory, but in practice it'd be too big a risk to even try it."

"Is this the one where he created a drug that he was trying to get approved by the FDA?" It's the closest one to public access.

"Yep. It looks like Oblitatrix, the drug he created to slow the spread of cancer cells, was tested on several cancer patients voluntarily after it passed all the tests on animals."

The uniform next to me checks his watch. There must not be much time left.

CHAPTER FIFTEEN

"Okay?"

"So I kind of abused my authority with the Ellsworth Medical Group and looked up old patients," she says.

"Yeah?"

"About a year ago, there was a Debra Mantel admitted to Ellsworth Cancer Institute for treatment. She died six months ago."

Mantel, as in Mitch Mantel. Maybe they're related. His roommate mentioned Mitch's dad several times but never his mom. Also, Isaacs told me that his drug had been used in small experimental settings. Was Debra included in that? Did she die because of it? Maybe Mitch blamed Isaacs for Debra's death and confronted him not knowing that Isaacs was Dust Storm. It's a leap, but it could be something. I'm desperate for anything right now.

"Any relation?"

"I'm still looking into that," she says. "But it could connect Mitch and Isaacs."

"That's what I'm thinking too. Was she included in the experiment?"

"Haven't found that yet, either. The journals don't list patient names and the list of drugs that was used on Debra is sealed. I'll see if I can find someone who can get into the records for me to confirm that she was part of Isaacs' test—"

"Time's up." The uniform takes the phone out of my hand and hangs it up on the wall. He leads me back to the interview room and shuts the door behind me.

Back at the table, I think about what Rachel found. If my hunch is right and Debra *did* die from Isaacs' drug, how would Mitch know he was behind it? And why was Mitch the one who ended up dead? Where does Abby fit into this?

The door swings open again and Detective Harkness steps inside.

"Have you had enough time to think?" She takes the seat

across from me again.

"Look, it's obvious you don't believe me, but you need to trust me. More people could be in danger."

She crosses her arms. "Give me one good reason I should believe anything you say. As far as I'm concerned, you're a John Doe because I know you're sure as hell not Ashton Cain."

Doubt creeps in that I'm wrong about who I am, but I push it away. "What I'm going to tell you is a little out there, but I promise you, it is one hundred percent the truth."

Harkness hooks an eyebrow.

"It also needs to remain anonymous," I add. "I'm telling you and *only* you."

"This is a murder investigation. Withholding information is grounds for arrest. Anything that you know that might be helpful needs to be shared with all involved parties."

"I know that and I want to help, but this could have bigger ramifications."

She shakes her head and rises to her feet. "If you're going to continue to proceed like this, then—"

"I'll tell you!"

That catches her attention, but she doesn't retake her seat.

Motioning to the mirror, I ask, "Can you please clear out the room back there and turn off any recordings?"

"I told you, all information needs to be shared—"

"Let me tell just *you* first," I plead. "If you think it's that important that it needs to be shared, I'll cooperate with any kind of recording of it. But just hear me out and weigh it for yourself first."

Harkness glances to the mirror and sighs. "I'll be right back."

In the silence after her exit, I fold my hands together in an effort to get them to stop shaking. This could be the end of it all for me. My newfound life could be in a six-by-eight foot room. If nothing else, hopefully it'll help put away Dust Storm. Somehow.

She returns and retakes her seat. "I asked Detective Watkins to step out of the room on the other side. All cameras and sound recordings have been disabled. You have five minutes. Talk."

"I need you to keep an open mind."

She turns up her hands. "What the hell? Why not?"

"Okay, I'm sure you've heard of the burning man or the man in red or whatever name they're calling him."

"Heat, I believe is what I heard on the news," she says. "Are you saying he's behind this?"

I shake my head. "No, he's trying to stop the person behind this."

She narrows her eyes and leans across the table. "And you would know this how?"

I swallow hard. "I told you I was having memory problems, right?"

"You mentioned it."

"Well, the truth is a couple months ago I woke up in a cave on the western mountain near the edge of the city. I had no idea who I was or how I got there. I *still* don't know how I got there. But after I woke up, I could…create fire with my hands."

She rolls her eyes. "Please don't tell me you were high and pulled out a lighter."

"No, that's not it. I—you know how Heat throws fire?"

More disbelief on her face. "Are you saying you're Heat?"

I put a finger to my lips. "Shh! And yes, that's what I'm saying."

Pushing away from the table, she says, "Okay. Well, thank you for wasting my time. We're done—"

"I can show you!"

Harkness studies me, curiosity brimming in her eyes.

"Watch." Raising my hand in front of me, I create a small ball of flame in the center of my palm.

Her eyes grow large and she sinks back into her chair. "Holy crap."

"Yeah."

"You're Heat."

Chapter Sixteen

Detective Harkness pushes away with her feet. The legs of her chair squeal on the tiled floor. "How are you—what—"

"I know." I stifle the flame. "It's weird."

"It's unnatural."

"Um. Okay." Best not to correct her when she's still in shock. "Detective, this is why I was talking to Sarah and why I was calling Mitch. I didn't realize he was the first victim when I tried calling him."

She seems to regain her composure and pulls the chair back to the table, trying to hide the fact that she just freaked out a bit. "Why was this case important to you? We've solved other murders since Heat—since *you've*—been around."

"I think the murderer is someone like me—someone with powers."

She shakes her head. "There was no evidence of a fire—"

"I know. This guy can turn himself into a cloud of sand."

"Like what happened to our victims," she muses.

"Exactly. We've been calling him Dust Storm."

"We?"

Oops.

"Yeah, me and a couple friends," I admit. "But they're only trying to help too. I don't want to bring them into this anymore than they have to be."

"Mr. Cain, like I said, this is a murder investigation. We need to have all the facts."

"But they didn't murder anyone, or even have anything to do with *my* investigation. Not really."

She huffs, but doesn't push it further. "So if you know who the murderer is, why haven't you gone after him?"

"Well, I know its Dust Storm, but I don't know *who* Dust Storm is."

"So you're right where we are."

"Basically. Maybe if we helped each other we could—"

"Absolutely not," she says. "I won't be corroborating with a civilian on any cases, especially this one."

"But I'm not just a civilian. I'm Heat." I give her a smirk.

"And as much as I appreciate what you've done for this city so far, I can't condone sharing sensitive information with you." She rises from her chair. "You're free to go. Just stay out of our way from now on, okay?"

"Wait," I call to her before she gets to the door. "I have my own list of suspects."

She turns and puts one hand on her hip. "And they would be?"

"Why would I share my information if you're not going to share yours?"

Turning, she reaches for the door again. "Goodbye, Mr. Cain."

"Mitch's mother had cancer, didn't she?"

Her shoulders slump and she turns around. "Where did you hear that?"

"I have my ways. But it certainly would connect our first victim and my current top suspect."

"Who is your top suspect?"

"You tell me yours and I'll tell you mine."

"Let me remind you, Mr. Cain, that I am a member of law enforcement."

"I'm very aware of your position, Detective, but I'm also protective of this information because I don't want any of your police officers to go after Dust Storm without my help."

She shakes her head. "No."

"They could *die*. Just take a look at Mitch and Abby. Not to mention my friend Melissa who was put in the hospital because of him."

"Melissa?"

"Didn't know about her, did you?"

Harkness gives in and retakes her seat. Again. "Who's Melissa?"

"I don't know how she fits into this exactly yet. I was hoping we could figure all of this out together. The longer we bicker, the more time Dust Storm has to go after his next victim. It might very well be Melissa, who is still hospitalized."

She lets out a deep breath. "Okay. Debra Mantel *did* die of cancer. Based off information we found on both Mitch and Abby's computers, we believe they were working on a formal proposal to deny the FDA approval of one Mrs. Mantel's treatments."

"Who were they writing to?"

"They hadn't sent any of their letters yet. They were smart. Figured their position would be strengthened with support from medical professionals. From what we gathered, they were still putting together that list."

"I wonder if Melissa was included."

"Why?"

"She worked for a pharmaceutical company."

"Doing what?"

I shrug. "She didn't really say."

"I'll have some of my guys check into that. Either way, we have a suspect in mind, but proving that he killed Mitch and Abby by supernatural means is not going to hold up in court."

"Are you thinking it's Dr. Henry Isaacs?"

She looks at me, stunned. "You really have done your homework on this, haven't you?"

"Well, I sort of work for him."

Her eyes narrow on me again. "You are one suspicious man."

"I'm helping right now, so leave it be. He told me he was working on a drug that would slow the rate that cancer spreads. We believe Debra was one of his test subjects. We're thinking Mitch blamed Isaacs for her death and confronted him, not knowing he was Dust Storm."

Harkness shakes her head. "I don't believe that was the case. Mitch Mantel was in one of Dr. Isaacs's lectures. He cleaned the basement where Isaacs's lab is. Mitch had multiple opportunities to confront him but witnesses from his class say that he was respectful of all his professors. Not to mention, Mitch had no history of violence, other than an attack last year with another classmate in which *Mitch* suffered injuries."

"Well somehow he ended up dead—and Abby too."

"Abby was his neighbor," she explains. "Her parents told us she was friends with Mitch and both families were close. E-mails and text messages between them indicate that she wanted to help after Debra died, which is why she got involved in the first place."

"Okay, so at least we know how Abby's connected."

"Plus, her name was included on the opposition letter Mitch was drafting," she adds. "We found it on his computer. And Abby's internet search history included links to articles about how to stop an FDA approval."

"Guess it pays to be law enforcement."

She smirks, then asks, "Did Dr. Isaacs give off any sort of

inclination that the murder was related to him?"

"No. Although he didn't seem happy about the fact that his drug was taking so long to get approved."

"That's the motive we're running with right now."

"I wonder if Isaacs got wind of Mitch and Abby's letter and that's why he confronted them. But no, Sarah said she and Abby were only apart for a few seconds when Abby died."

"We believe this was premeditated," Harkness says. "Not very well thought out, but thought out nonetheless. So there's credence to your theory that he heard about the letter from someone."

"Barry Murphy?"

"One of the researchers who worked in the lab next door?"

I nod. "I overheard him and Isaacs arguing this morning. Barry said something about backing out."

"Hmm. Sit tight." She gets up and leaves the room, returning a few minutes later with another manila folder. This one packed full with papers.

Pushing my folder aside, she opens the new one and flips through the pages.

"There were multiple investors for Oblitatrix," she says. "If Barry Murphy was—aha!" She pulls out a stapled packet of papers and skims through it. I recognize Dr. Isaacs's header at the top of the first page.

"Okay, there's a B. Murphy listed as one of the investors, which is odd. All of the other ones have their full names listed."

"So what is he hiding?" I ask. "I talked to him just before you brought me in."

She sighs and looks up at the ceiling. "Again with interfering with witnesses."

"Well, it's a good thing I did. He said that he and Isaacs have a shared investment. Something that Isaacs is in control of."

Chapter Sixteen

"Sure, Isaacs had to support his drug through repeated experiments and other tests," she says. "If he failed one of them, the approval would take longer or not even happen at all, depending."

"So killing the people who are behind the push to oppose the drug would mean that Barry would reap the rewards of his investment the sooner the drug could get to market," I speculate.

"Did he give you an alibi?"

"You didn't get one from him?" I ask.

"That's not what I said."

I sigh, tired of this game she continues to play. "He said he was at the gym the night Mitch died and I believe he was still in the basement lounge when Abby died."

"Well, another perk of my job is that I checked out his story," she says. "He *did* go to the gym around 7:30 that night, but security footage shows him leaving around 8:30."

"What was the estimated time of death?"

"Around 9:00."

"So he *could've* gotten back to EIT in time to kill Mitch."

"Especially if he can turn into a cloud, like you said," she adds. "However, there's something else."

"What?"

"Murphy had a daughter…with a woman who wasn't his wife."

My mouth hangs open. "Oh. I wasn't expecting that."

"Yeah. We tracked down the mistress and she confirmed he was there that night during the murder."

"So that means Barry's not our guy?"

"No, but it doesn't mean that he's innocent," she says. "Both he and Isaacs had something to lose if the drug didn't get approved. Barry, money; Isaacs, his reputation."

"You think they planned it?"

She shrugs. "I don't know for certain, but that's what we're thinking. We'll need to get him in here and get a confession out of him."

"What about Isaacs?" I ask. "He said he left at his usual time the night before and that he was late getting in the morning Mitch was found—which was also when Abby died."

"Part of that is true," she says. "He *was* late the morning Abby died. His secretary confirmed that. However, security footage shows him leaving EIT the night before shortly after 9:00."

"So he was there when Mitch died."

"Potentially," she says. "EIT is a big campus. He might've just missed the murderer."

"That's a big maybe. His lab is right next door to the one Mitch was killed in."

She shrugs. "I know, but sometimes you have to give people the benefit of the doubt until the evidence proves otherwise. I'm not going to deny that it's suspicious, though."

"Was there any footage inside the lab?" I ask. "Or in the stairwell where Abby died?"

"Nothing conclusive," she says. "The footage doesn't show the attacker, which makes me think that whoever did this knows the school well enough to stay hidden."

"Like Isaacs."

"Exactly."

"How do we prove that he did it?"

"Well, there are no murder weapons to connect his DNA to. No witnesses, and other than the security footage showing him leaving at night, there's no record of Isaacs in contact with Mitch that night."

"So we have nothing."

"No. I have an idea if we really are going to work together."

"Yeah?"

She points at herself. "We go after Barry Murphy and get him to confess—or share more of his story." She motions to me. "You go after Isaacs and figure out a way to prove that he's this Dust Powder guy."

"Dust *Storm.*"

"Whatever. Do you think you can do that?"

"I'll try," I say. "Let's go get them."

Chapter Seventeen

From an empty classroom on the fourth floor of the Herbert Building, I spot Dr. Isaacs coming down the hall. I followed him up here from his lab. He was in a department meeting for the last hour. Enough time for me to put on my Heat suit and come up with a plan to confront him. Hopefully Dust Storm doesn't make an appearance. That would put a lot of people at risk. Of course, it would also confirm that Isaacs is the one we're looking for and by then it'd only be a matter of time before we got him. The trouble is, so far I haven't been able to contain him as Dust Storm.

Hiding out behind the door of the classroom, I watch until Isaacs passes by. Reaching out, I grab him and pull him inside and shut the door behind us.

"Hey! Let me g—oh!" His eyes grow large when he sees me and the color drains from his face.

I lead him a few steps deeper into the classroom, out of sight of the window in the door.

Chapter Seventeen

"What is this?" He shrugs away from my grasp. "Don't touch me!"

"What, no sand this time?" I note how prominent his pulse is on his neck. His heart must be racing.

I've caught him.

"What are you talking about?"

"Your power," I say. "It's how you killed Mitch Mantel and Abby Adams. It's what put another girl in the hospital. All because of some stupid drug of yours that doesn't even work."

"Hey, what happened to those students was horrible, but I certainly didn't *kill* them. I barely even knew them! And I resent the fact that you're essentially calling me a fraud."

"Your words, but I certainly wouldn't disagree."

"That is a despicable accusation and I demand—"

I get closer, forcing him to take small steps back. "I demand you tell me some answers! You knew all three victims."

"I—I—I think I had Mitch in one of my lectures," he stammers. "But that's no reason to kill him."

"So you're saying you had no idea that he was fighting the FDA approval of one of your drugs? The one that makes you a fraud, in your words."

He grits his teeth for a moment, but ignores my comment. "Be that as it may, that's certainly no reason to kill him. And for you to suggest that the *way* they each died was something that is humanly possible is ridiculous. Nobody but *you* has abilities like that!"

With nowhere left to go, he backs into the back wall. I grab him by his shirt.

"Where did you get your powers?"

"I don't have any powers!"

"Yes, you do!" I raise my hand and conjure a ball of fire, holding it threateningly over him. If he won't turn into Dust Storm willingly, I'll have to scare it out of him.

Isaacs recoils, cowering away. This can't be the reaction of a guilty man. Not one who is under threat, at least. Am I making the same mistake I did a few days ago when I cornered Jim Jerrick? Is Heat really becoming that person who threatens confessions out of people?

The flame dissipates and I pound my fist against the wall behind him. I step away from him and walk to the door. Before I leave, I look over at him and catch a smirk on his face just before it turns back into a whimper.

He's guilty. And I'm not as dumb as he thinks I am.

———

LINDA LIVES ON Hickory Avenue, which is only a block over from the house that felt so familiar to me when I was walking this neighborhood several weeks ago. Now that I see it in the daylight, this area feels even more like home. Nostalgic, even.

After Detective Harkness confirmed that the Ash Cain I saw in the yearbook at the library disappeared in 1969, talking to Linda about what she knows is top priority. From the look Isaacs gave me, I know he's our guy but until he shows up as Dust Storm, I can't touch him. There's a lot of evidence that gives Isaacs motive, but nothing that proves that he killed those students. Until then, finding out who I am and where I come from is the itch that needs to be scratched. Especially because it's so weird.

The little yellow house that Linda calls home looks almost like it's pulled right from a storybook. The tall oak tree between the sidewalk and the street protects the front of the house from the beating sun, while still allowing plenty of light for the vibrant flower garden within the white picket fence.

When I was at the library, I spent most of my time looking into Linda's life through old *Ellsworth Gazette* newspaper articles. It's how I found out she retired in 2001 after teaching English for the Ellsworth City School District for thirty years. Her Facebook profile picture shows that she has a white lab. And, most shocking of all, she married Thomas Christianson in 1983 when she was 36. He taught math in the same school. I don't know if she's still married or if her husband has passed away, but I'm going to talk to her anyway. Even with Rachel and Perry's warnings, I have to find out who I was—or am.

Sticking to the opposite side of the street, I keep my distance so I can get a better look at her house without her thinking I'm a creep. Unfortunately, my plan goes right down the tubes when an elderly lady stands up straight from within the overgrown flower garden. She's wearing a sheer white shirt with a white T-shirt underneath and olive green pants. Her hands are covered by brown gardening gloves and she's holding a small shovel.

Seeing her stops me in my tracks. Not only because she startles me, but also because I recognize her. It's Linda, fifty years later. If the Ash Cain who disappeared is me and Linda and I are about the same age, she'd be in her early seventies by now.

Same age I should be.

Same age Arlus is.

My heart races and I know I should keep on walking as if everything is normal, but I can't get my feet to move. I'm frozen, facing her house and staring.

Noticing me, she turns and offers a friendly smile with a wave. Then her smile slowly fades as she studies me.

Recognizes me.

Finally, my feet decide to work. However, instead of carrying me further down the sidewalk, I'm crossing the street and walking *closer* to Linda. It's as if there's a magnetic force pulling me in.

"I'm sorry for staring," she says with another smile. "You just look so much like someone I used to know."

I nod. "Yeah, you look familiar too."

And she does. Now that I'm closer—the white picket fence the only thing separating us—I can see the beauty I saw in her before. The imperfections she's accumulated through the years are simply signs that she's lived. That she's moved on, despite my absence. I hope it's been a good life.

In our silence, I study her further. And I can tell she's doing the same to me. I wonder what she's thinking—if she recognizes me and if she is remembering the love we had for each other. Something I can only vaguely recall. Maybe she can help me remember.

"Would you like to come in for coffee?" she asks me. "I don't know if you need to get home or have any other plans, but I…I just feel like I…*know* you." She chuckles. "Well, maybe not *you*, but one of your relatives."

I look up at her house and then back to her. "What would your husband think?"

She takes it as a joke, even though my voice doesn't fluctuate at all. "Oh, I'm not married anymore. It's perfectly safe, if you don't mind a little dog hair."

Now I return the smile. "Yeah, that's fine."

She opens the gate for me and I step through, wondering if I'm making a huge mistake. Rachel and Perry didn't think this was a good idea, but as much as I know they care, they don't truly understand what I'm going through. I need to connect to my past. I need answers. Detective Harkness gave me a taste, but the only way I'm going to hear it all is from someone who was there.

When we step inside, an old white lab barks once when he sees me, but after I give him a good pet between the ears he settles down.

"Baxter behave," she tells him. "Sorry about that. He thinks everyone is here to see him."

I reach down and rub the old dog's side. "It's okay. He's just excited."

With the dog under control, I look around. The house is bigger than it looks from the outside. The walls of the front entryway are covered in floral wallpaper and painted white trim lines the corners of the room.

Chapter Seventeen

Linda leads me through her living room with a knitted afghan folded over the back of the couch. It's situated in front of a stone fireplace and a small TV in the corner. Several bookcases line the walls, filled to the brim with old tomes. Double stacked on the shelves and piled everywhere else—on the floor, along the mantel, under the TV, next to the couch, even on the end table near the couch—books have taken over the room.

Clearly, the woman likes to read. But I already knew that because I remembered. And that memory—and the fact that I remember it—brings a smile to my face.

The kitchen lies on the other side of a cased opening from the living room. It's small. About the same size as Perry's kitchen in his studio apartment. Only a little corner of counter space. Striped wallpaper in here. And orange glazed tiles on the floor. The large sliding door at the back of the room lets in most of the natural light for the two rooms.

Linda moves slow, but precise as she readies the coffee. She waves to the small black metal table with matching chairs in the corner. "Have a seat. This will just take a minute."

I sit and look around some more. There's a door to a bedroom through the living room and another door to a bathroom just inside the kitchen. Baxter curls up on a small dog bed in the corner and closes his eyes, content now that he sees we're staying in the kitchen.

"I apologize for the mess." Linda reaches for two mugs from a high shelf. "I ran out of room to put all my books a long time ago and I just don't have the heart to throw any of them out."

"I get it," I say quietly. "Do you need help with anything?"

"Oh no, dear," she tells me. "I've got everything covered." She pulls the carafe out and fills the two mugs. "Cream and sugar?"

I nod when she sets the coffee down in front of me. "Yes, please."

"Now, let's solve this mystery, shall we?" She takes a seat.

Dust Storm

Once again, I freeze. "Mystery?" Does she know about Dust Storm?

"Why we look so familiar to one another." She touches her chest with one hand and laughs quietly. "You looked like you just saw a ghost!"

I resume preparing my coffee. "Oh, sorry about that."

"Well, I'm Linda," she says. "Linda Page. What's your name?"

I clear my throat. "Uh…Ash. Ash Cain."

Her head snaps up from her coffee and she stares at me for a long time. I hold her gaze, hoping she'll figure it out on her own.

Instead, she blinks away tears and continues with her coffee. Quietly, she mutters, "Who are your parents?"

I take a careful sip. "I…I don't really know."

She doesn't contain her shock at all. "You don't know?"

"I've…uh…I've been having some memory issues for a while now."

Her lips quiver and her eyes well up again. Almost inaudibly she asks, "Ash? Is that you? *My* Ash?"

I lick my lips and look down at my coffee, not wanting to see her fall apart. "Yeah, Linda. It's me."

Chapter Eighteen

Linda's hand quivers as she covers her mouth. Her eyes remain locked on me, as if she's suddenly seeing me for the first time.

"How is this—where have you—" She's lost for words, yet a big smile appears on her face and tears well up in her eyes. "Can I give you a hug?"

I nod. "Sure, yeah."

We stand and she locks her arms around me tight. I remember the familiar embrace, the complete feeling of love I felt in those visions that transcended from our youth. It's the feeling of being whole because I'm with the one person who knows me better than anyone else on this planet.

And yet it's different. More a memory of a feeling than the feeling itself. Despite what my body might show, fifty years have passed since we shared that love. We've grown. We've changed. Even with all the nostalgia we feel, this isn't the same love we had all those years ago.

Finally, she lets me go and we retake our seats.

"How?" she asked pointedly.

I let out a deep breath. "That's a good question. I'm not really sure. All I know is, somehow I lost a few years."

She nods. "You've been gone fifty years this year. It was July 1969 when you vanished. I'll never forget it."

My eyes light up. "So do you know what happened? I was hoping you would."

"I'm afraid I don't," she says.

My face drops. "Oh."

"Not really, anyway," she adds.

I lean forward on the table. "Could you please tell me all that you remember at least?"

Linda looks away and wipes the tears with her napkin. "I was so heartbroken."

Reaching across the table, I squeeze her hands. "Linda, even through all of my memory issues, *you're* one of the first people I remembered. Very clearly, actually."

"You did?"

"One moment in particular I remember: We were sitting at our spot in the courtyard at EIT and I just felt…happy. In that moment, I knew just how much we loved each other."

She smiles and gives my hands a tighter squeeze. "Wait here."

Rising from her seat, she disappears into the living room. Baxter becomes alert, watching Linda move out of the room with his ears perked up. He looks ready to bounce out of his little bed at any moment. Linda comes back shortly after with a small framed picture and hands it to me.

"We were high school sweethearts," she explains.

The photo is of me with my arm around a much younger version of Linda at what appears to be a football game. We're seated on bleachers, me behind her, leaning in for the picture. We both have big grins on our faces. It's blissful. A real-life example that my memories are valid.

"We both went to EIT because we couldn't stand the thought of being away from each other," she continues.

I stand the picture up on the table so we both can see it. It's odd seeing myself in a photo I don't think I've ever seen before, but now that I am, I can almost remember it being taken. It's like a part of my memory is returning as I'm re-experiencing my past. Just as I hoped I would.

"I believe that was God's way of giving us four extra years together before you went away," she says.

I offer her a sad smile. "I'm still piecing together my past. I remember certain things, but not others and I can't quite figure out what everything that I do remember means. I was hoping you'd be able to tell me more about who I was—or rather, who I am."

The corners of Linda's mouth turn up as she thinks. "You were certainly a sweetheart, although you had a bit of a temper. But it was usually well-intentioned."

"How so?"

"You believed in doing the right thing—and you stood firm by that." She chuckles and stares off. "You used to even get in fights to defend someone who wouldn't stand up for themself." She glances over at Baxter and adds, "You were like a guard dog...*my* guard dog."

That explains why I'm so determined to help people as Heat—and also why I lost control with Jim Jerrick and Dr. Isaacs.

"How did we meet?" As soon as I say it, I worry that she might take offense to me not remembering, but she doesn't seem to notice.

"Ninth grade English class," she says with a smirk, relishing in the memory. "I'll remember it for the rest of my life. You, uh...had your favorite subjects in school." She shakes her head. "English wasn't one of them. At least not then. On the day we met, you didn't do the reading that was assigned for homework and since you sat right behind me in class, you tapped me on the shoulder to ask for help. You returned the favor later that day by helping me with one of our labs in chemistry. *That* was one of your favorite subjects." She stares off at Baxter again, still with the smirk. "I didn't realize it then, but you had me right from that moment. It was so simple and so sweet and it completely captured who you were as a person—who you *are*."

She turns back to me, but studies her nails. "Anyway, the next few classes you came up with every excuse to talk to me—even doing the assigned reading!" Linda chuckles at the memory. "Shortly after that, you asked me to one of the school dances and it was there that you asked me to go steady. And we were together right up until you disappeared."

She swallows hard, likely pushing away her sorrow. I decide to hold off on questioning her further about my disappearance right now.

"What else did I like to do? Was I in any clubs or anything? What was I taking at EIT?"

Linda shakes her head. "No clubs, really. You did a few sports, but nothing too seriously. When we got to EIT, you had so many hard classes that you didn't have time for much else. And yet you always found time for me. I tried not to push it, but I loved that you made sure we were a priority. You were always so sweet."

I can't help but smile. It's nice to hear good things about the person I was back then. "What was my major at EIT?"

"Criminal justice," she says. "You wanted to be a cop or something similar, which I was adamantly against. Like I said, you were always the guard dog. You just wanted to help people. After your brother joined the fire department, you volunteered for training and I didn't like that. I admired your drive, but I didn't want to ever get the phone call that said that you were…"

She covers her mouth and her eyes shut tight as her shoulders begin to shake.

I squeeze her hand. "When did I disappear?"

Pulling away, she wipes the tears from her eyes again before answering. "July 13, 1969. It was the most terrifying day of my life."

July 13th sounds familiar to me, but I don't give it much thought. Not while I'm in the midst of talking to Linda.

"What happened?"

"That was the day of the coal mine fire," she says. "We were having lunch at my parents' house when we heard. Both of your parents worked in the mine and you called Arlus because you wanted to help the fire department. You were about to start your training so you thought you could step in to help out. But he told you over the phone to stay away." She shakes her head. "You didn't listen. I begged you not to go, but you said you needed to be sure your family and everyone else was okay. Doing the right thing always came first for you."

I reach for her hand again but she pulls away.

"I watched the news as they reported and when they said there was an explosion, I waited, hoping I'd see you among the crowd at the base of the mine trail. I didn't, so I went down there myself to try to find you. There were *so many* people there, all looking for loved ones or trying to figure out what happened. I was there for *hours* searching for you but finally I had to accept the truth. You were inside.

"Shortly after it happened, I visited Arlus in the hospital—he was with the fire department in the mine. He said he was with you inside, but after the explosion, he couldn't find you. I wanted him to tell me more, but he wouldn't. He said he didn't know anything else, but I could tell that he knew more than he was letting on."

I'll bet he did.

"It was probably trauma," she says as an excuse for him. "The hardest part for me was that we never got a body to bury. That's how I knew that you were still out there, somewhere. And here you are! Somehow." Her voice croaks.

"Somehow," I murmur.

"What happened, Ash?" she asks.

I shrug. "I don't know. Honestly."

"You don't remember anything from the explosion?"

I shake my head. "I sort of remember running in, but that's it. I'm sorry."

She stares off toward the living room. "Something happened in that cave. I *know* it. Something that couldn't easily be explained. At the time, I knew in my gut that the love of my life hadn't died. I hoped and prayed that you'd return. I never lost faith, even when I tried to move on with other men."

"Your marriage?"

Linda leans her chin on her fists and looks at me. "Yeah. We were only married a short while. He was a good man. Smart, attractive, reasonably funny. Decent." Ever so slightly, she shakes her head. "But he wasn't you. And the woman I became when I was his wife wasn't me, either. She was a heartbroken person doing what she thought was right. My attempt to live out the dreams that you and I had set for ourselves. But it didn't mean anything because it became very clear that I didn't love him."

"What do you think happened?"

"What do you mean?" she asks.

"In the cave—or the mine, rather," I clarify. "You've been living with this for fifty years. You must've had your theories about what really happened to me."

"Oh, I've thought of every possible scenario," she says. "None of them make any sense. Disproven by one thing or another. The truth is that I don't know what happened. None of us may ever know. But one thing I've learned through my years of heartache is that sometimes you just need to accept things and carry on as best you can because otherwise, the grief will tear you to pieces."

Chapter Nineteen

So are you going to tell us the reason you insisted on having dinner in the hospital cafeteria?" Perry pushes around his mashed potatoes with his plastic fork. The mushy pile is slathered in dark gravy. Beside the cardboard carton its sitting in is another carton with French fires. Not the combo I would've picked, but he seems to like it.

"Well, I wanted to talk to both of you." I look between him and Rachel.

"Is this about you getting arrested?"

Perry starts choking and bursts into a coughing fit. "You did *what*?"

"Yeah. Right after we talked to Barry."

"How?" he asks.

"Yeah how?" Rachel adds.

"Turns out I didn't gain the trust of Abby's roommate like I thought I did," I explain. "She got in touch with Detective Harkness, who is the one who got Sarah to arrange a meeting with me so she could swoop in and arrest me." A thought strikes me. "Actually, they must've had this planned. When I saw Sarah in the café last night, she was very standoffish."

"Must be she had already made the deal," Rachel wonders.

"Back to the arrest. Are you fine now?" He dips one of his fries into his potatoes and pops it in his mouth.

"Yeah, sort of."

"Sort of?" Rachel asks. She cradles her fruit cup in one hand and her fork in the other.

"She didn't believe me that I was only trying to help."

"From her side it probably looked like you knew something," he says.

"Exactly. I think I might've even been one of their suspects. She also had questions about my identity."

Her face goes white. "Are they opening an investigation into you?"

I shake my head. "No."

"How come?" Perry licks the gravy off of each of his fingers.

"I…had to tell her I was Heat."

Both of them look at me with surprise.

"She *did* have a case against me with everything she found," I argue. "She laid it all out right in front of me and asked me questions I didn't even know the answers to."

"Like what?" She glances over at Perry wiping the last bits of gravy and mashed potatoes out of the bottom of the carton. "Would you stop? It's gone!"

He sucks on his finger and mutters, "Sorry."

"Well, for one thing," I go on, "I found out that I *am* from the 60s."

"And you verified that?" Perry asks.

"You saw the yearbook photo," I counter. "And Detective Harkness showed me a license picture from back then."

"Yeah, but that doesn't prove it was *you*," he says.

"He's right," Rachel adds. "After all we've seen, we can't just accept that until it's been fully vetted."

"It's been vetted," I say.

"How?" she asks.

"I went to see Linda today."

The two of them exchange worried looks.

"I thought you said you were going to stay away from her?" Perry asks.

"That changed when I got arrested," I say. "Harkness was asking me things I didn't even know—questions about *my past.* Luckily, when I told her I was Heat, that convinced her that I was trustworthy. At least, I hope it did."

"Yeah, let's talk about *that*," Perry starts.

"Not now," Rachel cuts him off. "How'd it go with Linda?"

I study the table, not ready to meet their eyes. "Good. I understand so much now, but there's still a lot that I don't know."

"Like?" Perry pushes, but Rachel swats at him.

"You don't have to tell us," she says. "As long as you understand, that's all that matters. Do you feel any better now that you've talked to her?"

"I do. About myself and where I come from."

"That's good." She gives me a sad smile.

"Did she recognize you?" Perry asks.

"Mm-hmm," I say with a nod. "She didn't seem too surprised, either. Actually, she was happy."

"Happy?" He hooks an eyebrow.

"That I came back to her."

Rachel straightens out her napkin. "That's good."

"And a little suspicious," he notes.

"She's in her seventies," she counters. "What's she going to do?"

He drops his voice and says, "So is Arlus Cain."

"For what it's worth, I believe that she told me everything she knows," I say. "The conversation was very genuine."

"That's good," Rachel repeats.

"I wasn't sure how she'd react," I say. "But I'm glad it went well."

We grow quiet. I think more about Linda and try to draw on the memories she stirred up. They're there, just not fully intact yet. Almost like a photo coming into focus. It just needs more time.

"So you're a 60s man?" Perry breaks into my thoughts. "That's rough."

I narrow my eyes. "Your parents were probably born in the 60s."

"But they didn't *grow up* in the 60s," he says. "There's a difference."

I roll my eyes.

Rachel clears her throat and smooths out her napkin on the table. "Are you going to see her again?" Her voice is small.

"I don't know," I say. "I would like to, only because I'm sure she has more stories, but you guys are right. It's probably best if I keep our visits limited."

"Damn straight we're right," Perry says. "But wasn't it weird seeing a girl you used to date all…*wrinkly*?"

"Sort of, but not really. I still feel a…connection to her," I explain. "And I can tell she feels the same way, but it doesn't really matter. So much time has passed. It's not like we'd start dating again."

"Ugh, could you imagine?" He slurps up the rest of his drink in his plastic cup. The last bits of liquid echoing off the inside of the cup.

"You know there's free refills, right?" Rachel says.

His eyes light up. "Really?"

"Yeah. Just show them your receipt."

"I'm gone!" His chair squeals loudly as he pushes it back and races up to the counter.

Rachel doesn't say anything, but it's very clear the Linda thing bothers her.

Chapter Nineteen

"I didn't mean to make you upset or anything," I tell her.

She waves it off. "Why would I be upset? It's your life. It's your past. You can do whatever you want."

"How's Melissa doing?"

"She's okay. Doing much better. Still coughing up some sand, though. Last I checked, the doctors were going to run some tests to check the extent of the internal damage."

I nod. "That's good. What does she think happened?"

"Apparently nothing related to the attack," she says, confused. "I think right now she's blocking it out. She told me she must've just breathed in something that blew off the top of one of those old industrial buildings. I'm sure she'll figure it out sooner than later."

"Neither of us saw it coming and Dust Storm doesn't really have a body, so maybe she didn't think it was an attack."

"Maybe."

"I should head up and see her now before visiting hours are over."

"That's a good idea." She fidgets with the corner of the napkin in front of her. Distracted.

"What's the matter?" I ask.

Shrugging, she says, "I'm okay."

"Rach, what's going on?"

She lets out a deep breath, eyes still locked on the napkin. "Evan and I had another fight."

"About money?"

"That's what started it, but it became so much bigger."

"I'm sorry."

"I'm just…not happy. And I don't know if it's with him or if it's my job and that's seeping over into my relationship, but I know I need a change. I can't keep doing this."

"Well, see where you can make adjustments," I offer.

"Yeah. A part of me wonders if I wouldn't be better off with a fresh, clean slate. But I think that would do more damage than anything."

"You'll never know unless—"

"Talk about a bargain!" Perry retakes his seat and sips up his refilled drink.

"Could you cool it on the enthusiasm?" she says. "It's just a drink."

"It's two drinks for the price of one, Rach," he says animatedly. "That's a big deal where I come from."

We laugh. It's what I need after the way the last twenty-four hours have gone for me. Hell, the last forty-eight, really.

"So tell us about your time in the Big House," he says. "I'm guessing you didn't get shanked."

Rachel shoots him another look.

"It was just the police station," I say. "I wasn't even booked."

"The coolness factor of your story is dropping," he says.

Rachel elbows him.

"Would you stop!?" he whines.

"This isn't a joke."

He sighs. "Sorry. How'd it go? Did this detective lady have any better idea who did it?"

"We pieced together who did it," I say.

Both of them lean in closer.

"Turns out they were following the same trail we were. She thinks it was both Isaacs *and* Murphy."

"Who?" Rachel asks.

"Someone Perry works with," I explain before going on, "The drug Isaacs is trying to get approved by the FDA is something that Barry Murphy invested in, but when Mitch Mantel's mother died from it, he and his neighbor friend, Abby, launched a campaign to block the FDA's approval. They asked people who work in medicine—including Melissa—to write up testimonies saying that the drug wasn't reliable."

"What does Melissa do?" Perry asks.

"Something at a pharmaceutical company. Graybar, I think she said."

"I've heard of Graybar," Rachel says.

"Are they good?" Perry asks her.

She shrugs. "They're thorough, I know that. They perform their own experiments to prove the quality of a drug before they start mass-producing it. If they had entered into any form of an initial agreement with Isaacs and Murphy, they would've found the same issues sooner or later."

"So what's the next step?" he asks me.

"Harkness has almost everything she needs to firm up her case against them. What she needs is proof that Isaacs is Dust Storm and she's hoping to get a confession out of Murphy. He has an alibi for that night, but she's going to question him some more."

"What about Isaacs?" Rachel asks. "How is she going to prove that he's Dust Storm?"

"She asked me to talk to him," I say. "And I did. As Heat. He put on an act and claimed that he didn't kill Mitch and Abby."

"But you know he did," Perry says.

"Right."

"So why aren't you going after him?"

"Because he thinks he bought time after our talk earlier today," I explain. "Maybe he thinks he's going to get away with it. And there are more people involved on his drug's opposition who are potential targets."

"But you don't know who," Rachel says. "Ash, you need to figure that out so you can protect them."

I shake my head. "Except, out of all three victims, there's one who survived and can still talk."

"Melissa," Perry says.

"Exactly.

"So that's why we're in the hospital," she says, a smile spreading across her face.

I nod.

"Very clever," she adds. "Oh, and this is perfect because there was something I was going to tell you before. Now that you know Isaacs is likely Dust Storm, it all makes sense."

"What is it?" I ask.

"You know how I told you on the phone I was looking through his medical papers?"

"Mm-hmm."

"Among the ingredients he listed in the mixtures he was creating, there were high amounts of mercury in every one."

"Mercury?" Perry asks. "Like what gave Ash his powers?"

She nods. "And probably Vernon too. We collected samples from the cave when we were studying you, Ash. Back at ESTR."

"Oh yeah. That was probably destroyed in the fire, though, wasn't it?" I ask.

"That's what I thought, but I found an article online that the salvageable materials they recovered from the destroyed lab was sold off to other researchers by River Valley, the lab's owner," she says. "Guess who bought some of the supply?"

"Isaacs," I offer. "In other words, my brother sold mercury to Dr. Isaacs, knowing that the heightened exposure would give him powers."

"Uh-huh," Rachel agrees. "Perry and I were careful when we extracted it, but with Isaacs not knowing the risks of its extra potency and handling substances like that on a daily basis…"

"He was more likely to be exposed," Perry finishes.

"Exactly," she confirms. "And if Ash, Vernon, *and* Isaacs all got their powers from the same source, what does that tell you?"

"That this isn't an accident," I say.

"So what are we going to do?" Perry asks. "If Arlus has created two supers already, he'll probably create more."

"That's what I'm thinking too," she says. "For now, though, Dust Storm is the one on the loose and killing people. The more pressing concern at this moment is to make sure that Melissa doesn't get hurt. So why don't we head upstairs to keep an eye on her?"

We get to our feet and head out of the cafeteria.

"Let's say we *do* get Isaacs in custody," Perry says, "regular jail cells aren't going to hold him."

"You're the tech genius." Rachel hits the button to call the elevator. "Any ideas?"

"Hmm…excessive heat could slow the particles down enough to keep them contained," he says. "Maybe a small oven-like room would keep him at bay. I don't know what kind of long-term effects it would have, but it's something to consider."

"Is that something you can create?" I ask.

He shrugs. "Yeah, I guess I could once I find the right thing to hold him."

The elevator doors open and a group of people step out.

"You should get started on that now," I tell him. "See if you can convert a microwave or an old oven or something. It doesn't have to be pretty—or big—it just has to work."

"Okay." He turns and heads to the exit. "I'll see you guys later!"

Rachel steps inside and holds her hand over the doors to keep them from closing. "Good luck!"

I take one step inside before my phone buzzes with an incoming call from Detective Harkness.

"Oh, I have to take this." I step back out into the hallway. "I'll meet you up there."

She gives me a nod and the doors close in front of her.

"Hello?"

"Heat?" Harkness says curtly.

"Uh, yeah, that's me." I'm not used to being addressed by that name.

"We got Murphy. He admitted that he and Isaacs planned the attack on Mitch because of the letter."

"Before or after Isaacs became Dust Storm?" I start walking toward the exit. If the police have Barry, I need to move in on Isaacs.

"Because of it," she says.

"Perfect, so it's confirmed that it's premeditated." I get to the front lobby and step outside. The sun is a large orange orb just behind the treetops.

"Except he only confessed to planning the attack against *Mitch*, not about Abby or Melissa. Claims he had no idea about them and both attacks came as a surprise to him."

"Those could've been Isaacs' own choices," I muse. "Unless Murphy's lying."

"I don't think he's lying."

"Well, we'll just need to get Isaacs' confession then. He should still be at EIT. I'll head that way now."

"You haven't approached him yet?" she asks.

"Not yet. I wanted to wait—"

"We don't have time to wait! This man is dangerous on his own, let alone the supernatural abilities he's equipped with. I want him downtown in thirty minutes."

"No, we're not ready yet! We have nothing to—"

"If he's not here in thirty minutes, we're moving in ourselves."

Chapter Twenty

Perry, you need to get to EIT *now*." I'm on the phone with him as soon as Detective Harkness ends our call. "I'm going to change and then I'll be there as soon as I can." I meander through the halls of the hospital, looking for a semi-private bathroom to change into my Heat suit, which is underneath my clothes.

"Why? What's going on? You just told me to—"

"I know what I told you, but that's changed." Finally, I find a bathroom in the basement, just to the right of the staircase. There's a large loading dock with the overhead door wide open, so I can sneak out of here undetected. "The police are going to move in on Isaacs without me if I can't get him before then."

"I thought you said they were working with you?"

I lock the door behind me, set the phone on speaker, and start pulling off my clothes, revealing the Heat suit beneath. "Apparently they're impatient. They know the risks, but—he'll kill them, Perry."

"Okay. How long do we have before they move in?"

"Half an hour." Pulling out the mask from my pocket, I fold up my clothes and search for a hiding place for them.

"It'll take me fifteen minutes to even get to the campus," he says.

"Well we need a plan!" My voice echoes off the tiled walls. Stepping on top of the toilet, I push up the ceiling tile and hide my clothes up in the drop ceiling.

"Stop panicking and let me think for a second," he says. "The device I was working on to dampen his powers is broken."

"By him."

"Either way, it's gone. We need something else. Essentially just an oven to contain him. Something that'll slow the rate at which he moves when he's Dust Storm."

"Isn't glass made out of sand?"

"That could kill him, Ash," he says.

"Maybe not. He'd have to be Dust Storm to even fit in any sort of oven, meaning that he'd be sand. We get him into an oven, crank up the temperature, and then he becomes glass. After that, we'd just need to break that glass into a million tiny particles again and he'd be sand."

"Maybe," Perry says. "The genetic makeup would be different."

"But he'd be the same person."

"In theory," he pushes.

"It's the only theory we've got!" I lean over the sink as Perry and I consider our next steps. Looking up, I catch my reflection in the mirror. Or rather, Heat's reflection. It's the first time I'm really seeing myself as this character I've created. It's kind of empowering, despite our present situation.

"Okay, so let's say that we can find an oven to contain him in, there's no way it'd be able to get it hot enough," Perry says.

"How hot does it need to be again?"

"Over three thousand degrees Fahrenheit."

Chapter Twenty

"So I'd need to add my own power behind it," I say.

"Except, standard ovens aren't made to withstand that temperature—especially from the outside. You'd break it and possibly even free him. It's not going to work."

"Well, Perry, we need to do something!" I shout again. "Time is running out and if the police make a move, they're all dead."

"Whatever you do, you need to make sure *at least* the building is clear."

"Ideally, I wouldn't move until the entire *campus* has cleared out. Chances are, that's where Isaacs is anyway."

"Clearing out the whole campus is not going to happen," he says. "Especially if the police are on their way. And I don't think you'll be able to lure him anywhere. Isaacs is smart. He'll know what's coming."

"Then what do you think I should do? We don't have a plan and we really need one right now."

"Did you ask Rachel?"

"No, I don't want to worry her," I say. "Not until I know what we're doing. You can call her and give her a head's up once we have a plan. I don't want Melissa to overhear anything."

Perry's end is quiet.

"Are you there?" I ask.

"The arts building," he says.

"What?"

"That's where you'll have to lure Dust Storm. It's right next to Herbert and I believe in one of the rooms on the second floor there's a kiln."

"Kiln?"

"For clay pots and stuff."

"You think that'll be strong enough to withstand the temperature?"

"Well, maybe," Perry says. "It's designed to contain exceptionally high temperatures. Most of them reach a maximum temperature of two thousand four hundred degrees."

"So not quite three thousand."

"No."

"Is it doable?" I ask.

"I suppose so. The fuel will have to be disengaged, so it'll solely be your power that's heating it. It's going to be hot."

Relief washes over me, followed immediately by nerves. There are a lot of ifs in this plan. How am I going to pull this off? Not to mention, we both just agreed that Isaacs won't likely follow me anywhere to get caught in our trap.

"Are you sure you're even going to be able to get the temperature up that high?" he asks.

"That's why they call me Heat," I tell him in an effort to give myself some confidence.

"I'm serious, Ash," he says.

"You're the one who did all those tests on me," I say. "What do you think? Can I reach that temperature?"

He breathes in a deep breath as he considers it, slowly exhaling to buy more time. "Maybe."

"Maybe?"

"The thermal radiation of a heat source that high will be enormous."

"In English, please."

"Don't stand too close to the fire because you'll get burned."

"But my body withstands flame all the time," I say. "Why wouldn't I be able to withstand this?"

"Because this is extreme," he says. "We're talking white-hot, burn-your-skin-off-within-seconds kind of heat."

"I think I'll be fine. The thing I'm worried about is getting everyone away so *they* don't get hurt."

"I'll have to work on that," Perry says. "Ash, this is risky. I'm not going to lie. With temperatures that high, the outcome can be a bit…unpredictable."

"It's a risk we're going to have to take."

"How are you going to get him inside?"

"Don't know yet. Any suggestions?"

"Not really. The kiln is front-loading, so that'll make it easier to get him in, but it still certainly won't be *easy*."

"I know, but he needs to be stopped." As long as I focus on that, I'll figure it out. "The kiln seems like the best way. I mean, I'll probably ruin it and everything else in the room, but at least a mutant killer will be off campus. I'll need your help."

"I already plan on being in your ear for this."

"I'll need prep help too," I tell him. "How close are you to campus?"

"Now I'm only about five minutes out."

"Good. Before I get to Isaacs, I'll need you to get the kiln ready."

"Ash, we're talking about *thousands* of degrees of heat. There's a safety feature on it that locks the door when it starts so people don't hurt themselves. Not to mention, the fuel source."

"Well, I'll need you to disable both of those," I tell him. "*Especially* the fuel source. We don't need the whole building blowing up."

He sighs. "I'll do my best."

"The kiln's going to be broken after this. No doubt about it. Doesn't make a difference if you break it beforehand. Not if it stops the bad guy."

He pauses again. "Are you sure you want to do this?"

"Why wouldn't I?"

"It's dangerous," he says. "You said Dust Storm can slip through cracks, right? The kiln's door will be sealed, sure, but Dust Storm might still be able to slip through. What if he does that while you're heating it up?"

I shrug. "It's a risk I'll have to take."

"And what about the fact that you're essentially killing a man?" he asks. "If he turns to glass, there might not be a way to go back from that."

"I tried the restraint method," I say. "It didn't work. And I tried talking to him too. *That* didn't work either. This is the only way."

"But now that you know it's Isaacs, maybe you can put new restraints on him."

"Perry, we don't have time for that. The police are on their way. Just get to the kiln and get it ready. I'm putting my comm in. Give me the go ahead when I can move in."

"Okay."

I sigh. "I don't like this idea either, but it's the only viable option we have."

"Oh no."

"What is it?"

"I can't get in."

I pick up my phone and bring it closer to my mouth, as if that'll bring me answers sooner. "Get in where? What's going on?"

"The police are all over campus."

Chapter Twenty-One

High above the city, I'm consumed in flames as I race to the Ellsworth Institute of Technology. Even as I'm crossing the river, I can see the flashing police lights. So much for the subtlety that Harkness promised.

At least if the police are there, they've likely already cleared the neighboring buildings to Herbert, meaning the arts building that Perry's trying to get into should be cleared too. Hopefully it's not on lockdown. I haven't heard anything to the contrary, though, so I'm hoping it's clear. Perry would tell me otherwise.

Landing right in the midst of a group of police cars draws attention to me, which is exactly what I want. When the flames around me dissipate, I call out, "Where's Detective Harkness?"

Most of the officers look my way with stunned expressions, but a few of them turn toward the Herbert building.

One of the officers points and says, "She went in about ten minutes ago with a small crew."

"And have you been in contact with them?"

"You need to ask the chief." He nods to a man walking up behind me.

"Who the hell are you?" The chief is stocky, dressed in a black suit that only adds to his aura of authority. He carries a walkie talkie in his hand and his suit coat flapping in the breeze reveals his badge and gun strapped to his belt.

"Why would you let your men inside when there's a known murderer in there?" I ask him.

"We're the police, it's what we do," he says. "Who the hell are you?"

"And have you ever confronted someone with powers like he has?"

"We haven't quite assembled our freaks and weirdos task force yet."

"You better hope that they're still alive," I say. "When was the last time you heard from them?"

"Our men are checking in from throughout the building."

"And Harkness?"

He lifts the walkie and says, "Harkness, do you read?"

We both look at each other, anxiously awaiting her response. Nothing.

"Harkness, are you there?"

I shake my head. "I don't like this. I'm going in. *Keep the rest of your men here.*"

"I can't authorize you to go in there," he says. "I'm sending in trained professionals."

Stepping closer, I get inches from his face. "Listen, if you send any more of your men in there, they're as good as dead. They don't have powers like I do. They're easy targets. Let's hope the ones that are already in there are still alive."

The chief glares at me. "I'll give you five minutes."

My feet start moving before I realize it. "Good. Keep everyone back! And make sure the arts building is clear too!"

Flames surround me again and I fly around to the opposite

side of the building by the main entrance and let the flames sub-side. Better to not draw anymore attention to myself when I go in. Hidden in the distance, I notice police snipers aiming their weapons in my direction. Hopefully they're not trigger-happy.

"Perry, what do you got?" I ask into my comm.

"I'm here," he says. "Just finishing up with the kiln."

"No problems getting in?"

"I had to sneak in through the tunnel system."

"No one is down there watching it?"

"Not that I could see."

Hopefully Isaacs hasn't figured that out yet. If Harkness and her men spooked him, he probably took off.

"Hurry up and get out of there," I tell him. "The police chief isn't giving me much time before more people come in."

"I'm doing the best I can," he says.

Pulling the door open, I step inside. The usually-bustling building is eerily quiet. Despite the setting sun still shining through the windows, I don't see anybody as I make my way down to the basement. The police seem to have sufficiently cleared everyone out. At least they helped with that.

Rounding the corner from the basement lounge, I head down the short hallway and can see the light in Dr. Isaacs' lab is still on. Makes me wonder how they cleared the basement without tipping him off. But then, if he's doing research—and he thinks that I've given up on him because of lack of evi-dence—he might not be on high alert.

When I step into the room, though, I see I'm very much mistaken. In the corner are Detective Harkness and two other police officers, each with their hands bound and mouth cov-ered with duct tape. A small cloud of sand hovers over their faces, threatening to suffocate them at any moment.

Isaacs is working at the center island. Several vials of liq-uid are set on the counter around various pieces of paper-work. He looks up when he sees me enter, as if he's expecting me. "Ah, Heat, there you are."

"The police have this whole building surrounded." I try to keep my voice even. Try not to show how scared I am that I won't get Harkness and her men out alive.

"Yes, I know." He motions to his hostages in the corner. "But, as you can see, they don't pose much of a threat to me."

"Let them go. They didn't—they're only doing their job."

"And I'm trying to do mine." He pours the contents of one beaker into another. "This job doesn't come with many thank yous. You try to do the right thing for mankind by finding ways to treat its ailments, but instead of gratitude you get people who try to not only discredit you, but ruin your reputation and your livelihood."

"You're talking about Mitch and Abby, right?"

"Not just them," he says. "Everyone who helped them."

"Like Melissa?"

Isaacs looks at me, brow furrowed. "Melissa…ah, that's right. Melissa Bowman. She's the one who's still alive, right?"

My hands tighten into fists. It's all I can do not to lunge at him. He barely even knows who she is, other than the fact that she was helping Mitch and Abby with their letter.

Switching tactics, I ask, "You're scared, aren't you?"

He laughs. "Scared? I'm untouchable!"

"What about your partner in all of this? Barry Murphy."

"Well, I assume that the authorities have already arrested him."

"And now it's your turn."

He smiles. "Do you think a set of handcuffs or a jail cell is going to keep me in place? I have more work to do."

"Scientific work or murder?"

Turning back to face the counter, he pours liquid from one beaker into another. It fizzles and smokes, but otherwise doesn't have a reaction.

"You and Barry only planned to kill Mitch Mantel, but *you*

decided to take matters into your own hands and kill Abby Adams and try to kill Melissa Bowman."

"I had more to lose," he says with venom in his voice. Apparently I hit a nerve.

"And Barry doesn't have anything to lose? He's a father, Isaacs. I'd say that's a pretty big thing to risk."

"What about me? My money, my career, my *reputation*?"

In my ear, Perry says, "It's ready. I'm waiting outside. It's Room 205. I left the light on so you know which one it is."

"Mitch and Abby had a lot of people helping them, Isaacs," I continue as if there was no interruption. "Are you going to kill them all?"

"If that's what it takes."

I need to get him moving. It's been well over five minutes, so the police are likely on their way in. I need to get Dust Storm to the kiln sooner than later so no one gets hurt in the process. Especially Harkness and the officers. If I can get Isaacs to make the first move, hopefully I can lure him away.

"Are you jealous of Barry? That he has people who'd miss him? I mean, you don't have a family. You're just a bitter, lonely old man."

"My work is all I need." He opens a drawer and retrieves a smaller vial.

"Your work? You mean, all the research that you've devoted your life to that hasn't amounted to anything at all? All that time you spent, all the sacrifices you've made, and what do you have to show for it?"

"That's enough." He shakes the vial frantically.

"Take a look at yourself," I go on. "You've lost control. Spinning in a downward spiral because you weren't good enough to come up with some beneficial research. You want to help mankind? Look what your drug did to Mitch's mother and all the other patients who were subjected to it. That's not to mention the *kids* you murdered."

Dust Storm

"Stop it!" he bellows.

"You're a failure, Isaacs. And now everyone knows it."

He pulls the stopper out of the vial and drops it in the beaker before tossing it my way. It crashes at my feet, shattering and mixing the liquids, causing a small explosion that sends me back a few steps. The next second Dust Storm swarms in the air and charges right at me.

Sand pelts my face and I burst into flames to keep it away. Shooting out of the room, I hover inches from the floor to make sure he's following. Dust Storm bursts from the room swarming around me, despite the flames.

I fall back, losing direction of what's up and what's down. All I know is that we're moving. I smack into a wall, then the railing of the staircase slams against my back, all while I'm swatting away the bursts of sand that attempt to penetrate my fiery barrier.

Dust Storm backs off and I finally get my bearings after the flames around me subside. I'm at the bottom of the stairs, still in the basement. Over the landing at the top of the stairs there's a large window outside. If I can—

The wind is knocked out of me as I'm smacked in the chest by Dust Storm, who has formed into a long, solid hunk of sand. Before I have a chance to catch my breath, my face is covered again and I'm forced to close my mouth to keep the sand out.

Uselessly, I swat the attack away, to no relief. The corners of my vision darken. I need air. Despite my mouth tightly shut, I begin to taste some sand working its way through. I need to get out of here.

My body erupts in flames again, but this time, I don't waste a second and fly straight up the stairs. Gasping for breath brings a mouthful of sand. It hurts like hell, but it's the only choice I have.

Now that I've pissed him off, Dust Storm is right on top of me, blocking my vision, causing me to crash right through the window at the top of the stairs and into the darkening night.

Outside with more space, the flames keep Dust Storm at bay long enough for me to fly off without fear of hitting anyone or anything. Long enough for me to properly fill my lungs again, too. I'll need all the strength I can get if we're going to keep this fight up.

Below, fire trucks pull into the parking lot closest to Herbert, right next to the cadre of police cars. I might need them later if something goes wrong with this kiln thing. I wonder if Perry called them or if the chief did.

"Get him to the art building!" Perry says in my ear.

"I'm trying! Tell the police Harkness and a few officers are in Isaacs' lab. He's right on top of me, so it should be clear."

"But won't that—"

"Figure it out! I'm busy!"

Not wanting to go inside and risk getting trapped in a tight space, I fly around the outside of the arts building in search of Room 205. Luckily, Perry left the light on so it doesn't take long to locate.

I fly straight toward it, turning at the last moment so my shoulder takes most of the impact of the glass. The flames disperse just as I collide with the window. The force sends me crashing into one of the large work tables in the center of the room, shards of glass flying all over.

Slowly, I get to my feet, noting how eerily quiet it's suddenly become. My collision course with the table has knocked the wind out of me. Again. I gasp for air, hoping I'll have enough time to regain some strength before Dust Storm shows up. I'm getting sick of not being able to breathe.

The quiet continues.

Maybe Dust Storm anticipated what I had planned. Dr. Isaacs is brilliant and he's worked at EIT a lot longer than I have. Surely, he must've figured out what my plan was.

Stepping over shattered glass, I make my way to the broken window and peer out into the sky, looking for any trace of sand—or even Dr. Isaacs. If he's not coming, I need to get back to Herbert. Maybe he saw the officers from the parking lot running in to free Harkness and—

Somewhere, I hear the faint sound of rustling sand. Almost like a rattle snake's tail warning of an imminent attack. Through the window, my eyes scan up, down, side to side, all over what I can see of the campus from this vantage point but I don't see any sign of him.

Suddenly, I'm pulled backward. The rustling sound intensifies as the room fills with sand quickly. Another extension of Dust Storm's power. Before I realize what's happening, the sand has multiplied until I'm buried up to my knees, unable to move.

Opening my palms, I shoot flame down around near my feet. While it subsides a little, sand from behind me falls into the place of my attack.

Up to my waist now, I start digging my way out, trying desperately to free myself. With all of the energy I can muster, I try to wiggle my feet, twist my body, do *something* to alleviate the pressure of the sand.

It's no use. With my arms raised high in the air, the sand reaches my neck. I can't move. I'm stuck.

"Perry! Help!"

It's my last chance of survival. I barely get the two words out before I'm forced to shut my mouth as the sand rises higher, threatening to end my air supply once and for all.

Chapter Twenty-Two

I struggle in the packed sand to no avail. It's too heavy for me to move and I'm only wasting air supply by trying to get free. The lack of oxygen immediately stifles my efforts to burst into flames.

"What's going on?" Perry asks. "I can't see anything from the security camera in the hall. The door's closed. Wait, is that… sand on the floor? Ash—Heat, are you in the art room?"

I can feel my heartbeat in my ears as my body is slowly compressed from the weight of the sand. If I open my mouth at all, Dust Storm will strike and I'll end up just like Mitch and Abby.

"Answer me!" he shouts. "What do you need?"

Nothing. I can't say a single thing. I can't *do* a single thing except wait to die.

"Hold on."

With my lips tightly pressed together, I scream in the back of my throat. It's the only way I can think of to let him know that coming in here is a bad idea. Nobody else can face off against

Dust Storm

Dust Storm. Except maybe the Gatekeeper, but his involvement is debatable as it is. Why does my brother hate me so much?

Focus, Ash, I tell myself. *If Perry sends in the police to help, they're all going to die because you got yourself stuck.*

The sand begins to shift. Retreating, shrinking away. After a little while, it slides away from my face and I gasp for air. The further the sand subsides and disappears, the more I feel water raining down from the ceiling. Perry must've set off the sprinklers. Slowly, my arms are freed and eventually, the rest of me.

I breathe in deep breaths as quick as I can, knowing I only have a short window before Dust Storm strikes again. My vision is blurry and my limbs shaky from lack of oxygen, but I need to move.

Scrambling to my feet, I rush to the kiln and open the door. Snatching up a large poster board from the floor—something that must've been on the drying rack before Dust Storm swarmed in—I rip it in half and toss it inside the kiln, sending a ball of fire inside with it. Grabbing at other ruined pieces of art, I toss them in the kiln to help feed the flame. Just long enough for me to get Dust Storm inside.

The small patch of wet sand still stuck to the floor near the kiln dries as the heat from the fire grows. With everything I add to the kiln, the fire burns brighter and the sand lifts from the ground to swirl in the air.

Turning, I note small patches of wet sand all over the room.

"I don't think we need the kiln," I say into the comm. "The water seems to be subduing him. If we can just keep the sand wet, it looks like it'll be enough to—"

Something smacks into me hard from behind. Turning, I see the sand has taken shape of something that almost looks human. Whatever it is, it has its fists raised. The closer it gets to the heat radiating from the giant oven, though, the more the mound dries, sending particles of sand swirling into the air, joining the other swirl.

Chapter Twenty-Two

"What's going on?" Perry asks.

"Bad idea!" I shout back. "There's two of them now!"

Opening my palms toward the large mound, I shoot a stream of fire at him. Hopefully, if I dry him out, it'll all just become one big swirl. At least that way, I'll know how to stop him.

The swirl hovers in the air as the drying sand continues to join it, creating a bigger and bigger cloud of sand.

"Okay, we might have a new problem," Perry says.

"What's that?"

The swirl moves toward me as the last sand mound dries up. I run around the room, encouraging a chasing game. If I can get Dust Storm moving fast enough, he won't be able to stop as he vaults toward the kiln. And whenever I pass by it, I can feel the heat. It's almost time.

"Do you have the kiln's door open?"

"Yeah, I need to get him in there."

"It's nowhere near hot enough," he says.

"Give me a sec!"

I hop over the shattered remnants of the table that caught my fall on the way in and nearly slip on another ruined poster on the floor.

"You've gotta move quick!" Perry says. "I added a thermometer on the back side of the kiln so I know how hot it is when you blast it. With the door open the flame is dying."

I sprint toward it, feeling a few particles of sand poking at my back.

Really close. The room isn't big, but I run the length of it, trying to pick up speed.

At the last moment, I dive to the ground right in front of the kiln. Just as I'd hoped, most of the swarm that makes up Dust Storm flies right into it.

Quickly, I slam the door shut and lock it.

"Got him in."

"Good," Perry says. "You've got a lot of work to do."

"How hot?"

"To turn sand into glass? Three thousand ninety. And it needs to stay that consistent for a while."

Opening my palms, I shoot fire at the outside of the kiln. Hopefully that'll bring up the temperature. It's the only move I have now that the gas line has been disconnected.

"How long is a while?"

"At least ten minutes," he says. "Are you timing this?"

"No, you do it."

"I'm tracking the temperature now," he says. "You just broke a thousand. It's getting hot in there. Is he escaping?"

"Not that I can see." All that's within my view is the flame extending from my palms to the kiln, licking off the sides. "There isn't a way for him to escape inside there, is there?"

"I suppose maybe the gas line, but I capped that off to make sure that there wouldn't be any explosions."

"Good thinking."

"Fifteen hundred now. You're getting there."

"Is Harkness safe?" I need a distraction. Something to focus on so I don't think about how draining this is.

"Yeah, she and the two officers managed to free themselves before reinforcements got there."

"Good. What are we at now?"

"Two thousand."

"Almost there." Sweat rolls down the side of my face. The room is hot. *Really* hot. Not only that, but increasing the temperature of *my* flame takes more out of me than I thought it would. I'm beginning to have doubts that I can sustain this for as long as I need to.

"Two thousand five hundred," he says. "How are you holding up?"

"I'm fine." My arms are getting tired. It's not even up to the right temperature yet and I'm already getting weak. Nearly suffocating a few minutes ago—and running around the room—

didn't help with my exhaustion any. "Did Harkness or anyone say anything to you?"

"No, she's still getting checked out. It's a circus here."

"I bet."

"Three thousand. You're doing great, Heat."

I must be holding up better than I feel.

"Where are you?"

"In my car," he says. "I'm parked kind of in the middle of the street that leads to the school, but everything else is blocked off. It's the closest I could get."

"Good." At least he's safe. "Does Rachel know what's going on?"

"Yeah, I texted her," he says. "My phone hasn't stopped buzzing since, but I've been a little preoccupied with you. Okay, you're at three thousand ninety. Starting the clock now. How's it looking?"

Holding my stance and making sure my flame keeps coming, I look at what I can see around the blast. The floor and the wall behind the kiln are charred black. Some of the errant artwork that clings to the drying racks is in flames. Not that I'm surprised with a three thousand degree fire burning only a few feet away. I just hope the building doesn't catch.

"The walls are scorched," I tell him. "There are several little fires everywhere. It *smells* really bad."

"Yeah, likely from plastics and other toxic chemicals released from the heat. Probably burning off the side of the kiln and anything else that's close."

"Something is trickling out the bottom of the door!"

"What's it look like?"

I narrow my eyes and look closer. "It's...dripping."

"That's good. That means the sand is liquid now. You're at two minutes. Eight more to go."

Fatigue is beginning to set in. I'm not sure I'm going to make it another eight minutes. I wonder if Dust Storm has melted enough so that we can apprehend him. Maybe the police can keep him locked in a controlled environment to keep him at bay. But then what if something happens—power outage, fuel shortage, fire—and he escapes? It'd be like poking a beehive.

"Six minutes," Perry cuts in. "How are you feeling?"

"Tired," I say. "Do you think he'd be okay if I stopped? I don't want to kill him."

"You're not killing him," he says, convincing me now. "Only changing his form."

"So there's a chance he can return to his human form?"

"Ash, you said it yourself: if we grind him up into fine pieces, we're essentially turning him back into sand."

"I know, but now I'm panicking that the police aren't going to see it that way."

"If you weren't doing this, they'd be dead."

Another droplet of sweat runs down my face. We've had this conversation already, but at least he's keeping me talking. Without him, I'd be a pile on the floor. Hell, without him, Dust Storm would've suffocated me. I owe him more than I can ever repay him.

"Is the fire department on standby?" I ask.

"I don't know. Why? Do you think you're going to burn the place down?"

"It's crossed my mind."

"Well, the structure is likely mostly made from bricks and other non-combustible materials, for *this* same reason. I mean not this reason, but regular fires and stuff. If anything's going to catch it'd be the furniture. Of course, if that gets hot enough, it *could* cause issues with the structure—"

"Perry?"

"Yeah?"

"That's not helping."

"Oh. Sorry."

I try to wrap my head around the fact that I'm basically

ending someone's life because he killed two people. Is that justice? Two wrongs don't make a right. But this is the only way to stop him. Containing him in glass isn't exactly *killing* him. Like we've discussed, we're just changing his form. It just… doesn't feel right.

"Four minutes."

Perry's voice startles me and nearly makes the fire stream sputter, but luckily I hold it.

"I'm not sure about this."

"Are you okay?" he asks. "Are you going to pass out or something?"

"No, I'm having second thoughts about what we're doing to Dust Storm—to Dr. Isaacs. He's a person."

"So were Mitch and Abby. So is Melissa. He killed people, Ash. Because he didn't get his way. You're doing this for them because you can stop him from hurting anyone else. You've got this, Heat."

His words help convince me, but the immense energy it takes to maintain this level of exertion takes a toll on my body. My knees are going weak and the oppressive heat is making breathing difficult.

I wonder what the intensity is like outside of the room. Are the police clearing everyone back away from the building? Did they call the fire department? Do they suspect that I'm trying to commit arson? Or do they understand that I'm using my ability to help them?

"How's it out there?" I ask Perry. "I need a distraction."

"Several firetrucks just showed up," he says. "I can't really see much else. Everyone's just standing—wait, no. I just saw a few firemen run in."

Dammit. I don't need them getting anywhere near this room. Not right now.

"One more minute," Perry says. "You've got this!"

In my head, I count down from sixty, but when Perry chimes

in to tell me there's thirty seconds left, I lose concentration. Sweat continues to run down my face, running into my eyes. I blink them away.

"Ten…nine…eight…"

I wonder if I'll collapse when it's over. How long will it be before the room's cooled enough for someone to reach me? And how long before I wake up? Am I draining my life away by feeding this flame for this long?

"Three…two…one! You can let up now."

Despite wanting to quit several times, I find it hard to stop cold turkey. Instead, the flame slowly subsides as I withdraw the energy. Afterwards, I stumble back and lean against one of the work tables that's not scorched black. One corner even has a small flame. I cover it with my hand and stifle it.

My chest heaves. My extremities feel almost numb. But I'm here. I survived. It's over. Most importantly, Mitch and Abby's killer has been stopped. And short of anyone grinding him down, Dust Storm will forever be encased as glass.

————

"WELL, THAT'S ONE way of stopping him," Detective Harkness tells me out in the parking lot. She's wrapped in a blanket from the ambulance. There's a butterfly bandage over the gash on her forehead and I notice the abrasions on her wrists from the binds, but otherwise she seems okay. "Did quite a bit of property damage. The school might want to press charges."

I glance at her. I'm leaning against one of the police cars, still trying to slow my heart rate. I wonder how close I came to passing out. I refused to let any of the paramedics take a look at me. Whatever's going on with me is a unique beast because of these powers. Besides, I don't want to take off my mask.

"Would *you* press charges?" I ask her.

She studies me. "No. God knows we couldn't have pulled off

what you did. You did good. And I actually owe you an apology."

"For what?"

"You told me that we wouldn't have been able to handle him on our own and you were right," she says. "I was being stubborn and I put people's lives at risk. So I'm sorry for not listening."

Behind the mask I grin. Luckily, she can't see it.

"Are you going to charge him?" I point up to the building. The firefighters are still scoping it out, making sure there aren't any active fires or any accidents waiting to happen.

"I'm sure there will be paperwork," she says. "We're going to have to come up with a new system for criminals brought in by you."

"Why's that?"

"Uh…there isn't exactly a standard protocol for men who are brought in as glass statues."

I chuckle. "I guess that's true. As long as you get his nick-name right."

She hooks an eyebrow. "Nickname?"

"Dust Storm." I nod over to Perry off to the side. He's on the phone with Rachel, explaining everything. "He wouldn't be happy if you got it wrong."

Harkness glances back at him and then turns to me. "Part of your team, is he?"

"You have to keep this just as guarded as my identity," I plead. "We're only trying to help. And obviously, you needed our help."

She chews on her bottom lip as she stares at me. "Okay. I mean, you did help us get the killer. So thank you for that."

"You're welcome. Maybe next time you'll listen to me in-stead of running into something like this yourself."

"Next time?" she asks. "You think there will be a next time?"

"Oh, I'm sure there will be. And I think it'd probably be bet-ter if we found a way to work *together* on these types of cases from the get-go."

"I don't know if that's something I can commit to," she says. "Protocol says that—"

"Screw protocol," I cut her off. "We both want the same thing: murderers off the street. Guys like Dust Storm just require…a certain specialist."

She chuckles. "And I take it you think you are that specialist?"

I motion up to the arts building. "I just turned a man into glass! So yeah, I think I am."

Laughing again, she says, "You've got a point. So I'll tell you what, next time a case like this pops up, we'll be in touch."

"Sounds like a plan." I extend my hand for her. "Thanks."

She shakes it. "No, thank you. Honestly, you were a big help."

That makes me feel incredibly proud.

"Take care of yourself, Heat."

"You too, Detective."

CHAPTER TWENTY-THREE

ey, how're you feeling?" I ask Melissa when I visit her the next morning.

"Better," she croaks. "My throat is still sore. Been having ice cubes and ice cream to help soothe it."

I make a face. "I'm sorry."

She shakes her head. "Don't be. I love ice cream!"

With a sad smile I say, "That's not what I meant."

"I know. But it's not your fault."

I want to tell her that her attacker is taken care of. I want her to know that she doesn't have to worry about anymore supernatural attacks. But that would mean that I would tell her that I know more than I'm supposed to.

Melissa's attention shifts to the TV hanging on the wall across from her bed. I turn and notice myself—Heat, rather—on the screen. It shows me in flame, bursting out of the Herbert building with Dust Storm on my tail. The camera shakes, but the end of the clip catches me slamming into the window of Room

191

205 in the arts building. Dust Storm lingers, but whirls around to another entrance.

It cuts to a woman with short blonde hair sitting behind a desk in the newsroom. She's surrounded by a light blue background and she stares at the camera with a serious look.

"Turn it up," I say to Melissa.

She reaches for the remote and a bar appears at the bottom, counting up from zero.

By the time I can hear the audio, Detective Harkness is on the screen with a microphone held up to her mouth.

"I just want to thank Heat for his help in stopping this…*being* that we've been calling Dust Storm," she says.

I smile. Perry will be happy.

"Truly, without him, Dust Storm could've potentially hurt so many more people," she goes on.

The screen cuts back to the newsroom and the blonde woman says, "No word on who exactly Dust Storm is, but the Ellsworth Police Department released a statement saying that the individual is in custody."

"It's crazy, isn't it?" Melissa asks me.

"What is?"

"Well, do you think that this Dust Storm person—thing—is what happened to me?"

"What do you think?"

She shrugs. "The doctors keep telling me there's sand in my lungs. I just thought that's what they were calling it. It didn't make sense, but I can't deny the pain." Almost on cue, she breaks into a coughing fit and reaches for her water. When she's done, she goes on, "Ash, you were there. Did you see that Dust Storm person attack me?"

My stomach drops. "There was a lot going on and—"

"Just answer the question."

"Yeah, I think it was."

"Oh." She considers it for a moment and then adds, "Weird."

Chapter Twenty-Three

I chuckle nervously. "Yeah. Weird."

"Who do you think it really was?"

I shrug. "Does it matter?"

"Well, yeah," she says. "I would like to know *why* I was attacked."

"At least he's taken care of." Hopefully she'll find out eventually. I can't blame her for wanting to know the truth.

"And is he going to pay my medical bills?" She breaks into another coughing fit and her face contorts in pain. Her fist pounds at her chest as she lurches forward. After several phlegmy coughs, she takes several sips of water and lies back down.

"You shouldn't talk," I tell her. "I'm sorry. I shouldn't have started asking you questions."

Melissa waves toward her and I step forward. She slips her hand in mine and squeezes.

"I had a good time on our date," she says softly. "Besides the ending."

I pull a chair closer and take a seat. "I should probably talk to you about that."

Her brow furrows and she tries to pull away, but I hold on.

"It's not anything bad," I say quickly. "I'm just—I had a lot of fun with you too. And I like you. I really do, I'm not just saying that. But I think, with some of my…memory problems, that it's probably best for me to take some time for myself right now. Not see anyone, you know?"

"I could tell."

"How?"

She shrugs. "You seem conflicted. Hesitant to allow yourself to enjoy life. Like something heavier is weighing on you. I don't know if it's another commitment to someone else or what, but I agree that it's probably not fair to start anything until we *both* know for sure that it's what we want."

Melissa reaches for her cup and downs the rest of the water.

"I'm sorry," I say.

"Don't worry about it," she says. "It's fine. We went on one date. It was fun, but if there are other things going on with you right now, then you need to focus on that. Take your time. When you're ready, give me a call and see where I'm at. Maybe we can go on another date then."

I lean back, amazed that Melissa's taking this so well. It's not like she just went on a date that didn't go anywhere, she went on a date that put her in the hospital that *still* didn't go anywhere.

But I can't pursue a relationship with her simply because I feel bad about what happened. Because she's right. I am conflicted, weighed down by all that's happened in my past and what that means for my future. On one hand, I still have deep feelings for Linda, but I know that things will never be the same again between us. After all, those feelings are for the Linda from the 60s, not today. On the other hand, I need to figure out what exactly happened to my parents and why my brother hates me so badly.

"It's probably for the best." Melissa cuts into my thoughts. "My doctor said that there's nothing more he can do for me and recommended that I see a specialist."

"That's great! Maybe they can really help you."

She nods. "I hope. It's just…it's in New York City."

"Oh."

"Yeah. So you're right, this isn't going to work right now. And not just because of what you've got going on. I've got stuff going on too."

"That's true. I want you to get better." I squeeze her hand again.

"I will. It's just going to take a little bit. It is a little sad that this is ending before it really got a chance to start, though."

"Yeah, but it wasn't for lack of attraction."

She smiles. "Definitely not. And who knows? Just because the timing's not right at this moment, doesn't mean that things won't work out in the future. Don't be a stranger, Ash. There's a lot more about you I'd love to get to know."

Chapter Twenty-Three

———

THE GRASS IS wet from the first rainy day of the season. Fall is coming. The chill in the air is a good sign of that. Despite the drizzle, I kneel in front of the stone anyway, feeling the moisture soak into the knees of my jeans. The stone is modest. Simply a marker that's nearly buried in the ground that reads:

AMY ELIZABETH CAIN
- BORN APRIL 26, 1971 -
- DIED JANUARY 1, 1991 -

"Hi Amy." I chew on my bottom lip, feeling a little self-conscious about talking to the ground. But I owe it to her. She's family. Besides, the rainy day guarantees that no one else is around.

"Uh…I'm your uncle, I guess." I clear my throat. "I'm sorry this is the first time I'm seeing you. But, from what people tell me, and from the year you were born, I guess I wasn't around at all in your life. Anyway, I've known about you for a few weeks now. Well, since I've been out of the cave. I looked you up after your father told me he and I were, uh…brothers. It's weird."

I pull a few pieces of grass out of the ground and rub them between my fingers until the water runs down my hand.

"Anyway, I know I should've visited sooner. I just couldn't bring myself to see you because…well, because of who your dad is. I know—somehow—that we're family, but from what I've seen of him so far, there's no brotherhood left between us. He's…not a nice person. And, if I'm being honest, it makes me more than a little afraid that *I'm* not really a nice person because *he's* not a nice person. But that's not the story I've heard about myself, at least. So hopefully that's true."

I shake my head and study my fingers kneading a new piece of grass. "I know, it's probably stupid, but that's what's been going through my mind these last few weeks. At least whenever I let myself think about it. I'm going through a rough time right now, Amy. I don't feel like myself because I don't know who I am. I have different people telling me different things and I don't know what's right and what's wrong. I just really wish you were still here because I would love to know what kind of person *you* were."

Looking down, I notice the veins in my arms, accentuated by the muscle beneath them. I absently reach up and feel the smooth skin on my face. Rachel and Perry estimated that I'm in my early twenties. Linda says I disappeared four years after I graduated high school, meaning I'm probably around twenty-one or twenty-two. Amy wasn't even twenty when she died.

"I wish I was there when you were growing up. I wish we were friends. But unfortunately we never met because you weren't born yet when I…disappeared. I think that's a real shame. But I still feel a connection to you because—again, somehow—we're family. And right now, with everything that's going on, I really could use a family."

When Ash gets a phone call from Detective Jenna Harkness, he knows he's in for a whirlwind. She tells him an officer brought in a crazy man who might be of interest to him.

The man thinks it's 1969.

But when Ash listens in when Harkness interviews the man—who identifies himself as Donald Douglas—he isn't convinced that there's much of a connection. That is, until Douglas lays eyes on Ash and spits in his face.

The team soon discovers that Douglas is the latest hitman hired by the Gatekeeper to kill Heat. But they still haven't figured out a way to stop the Gatekeeper and keep him contained under police supervision. And unlike Heat, he's willing to change history to settle the score.

———

Available in ebook, paperback, and audio!
DavidNethBooks.com/Heat

More by the Author

To find the rest of the author's books visit
DavidNethBooks.com/Books

Subscribe to his newsletter to be the first to know of new releases and special deals!
DavidNethBooks.com/Newsletter

If you enjoyed the book, please consider leaving a review on Goodreads or the retailer you bought it from. Reviews help potential readers determine whether they'll enjoy a book, so any comments on what you thought of the story would be very helpful!

About the Author

David Neth is the author of the Heat series, Fuse series, the Under the Moon series, and other stories. He lives in Batavia, NY, where he dreams of a successful publishing career and opening his own bookstore.

———

Follow the author at

www.DavidNethBooks.com
www.facebook.com/DavidNethBooks
www.instagram.com/dneth13